CHOCOLATE BUNNY BETRAYAL

A HOLIDAY COZY MYSTERY
BOOK FIVE

TONYA KAPPES

D1607630

TONYA KAPPES
WEEKLY NEWSLETTER

Want a behind-the-scenes journey of me as a writer?
The ups and downs, new deals, book sales, giveaways and more? I share it all! Join the exclusive Southern Sleuths private group today! Go to www.patreon.com/Tonyakappesbooks

As a special thank you for joining, you'll get an exclusive copy of my cross-over short story, *A CHARMING BLEND.* Go to Tonyakappes.com and click on subscribe at the top of the home page.

PREVIEW

Darren leaned in just enough to get my heart racing and my mind believing he was about to kiss me. Right there. In front of everyone.

A bloodcurdling scream made us jerk apart and look to see who was in desperate need of help.

The seven Easter Bunnies scattered in different directions. Make that six, because the one Mama was standing over lay flat on his fluffy back. Colorfully decorated Easter eggs had spilled out of the white basket and were strewn all around the costumed person auditioning for the part.

Mama brought her hands over her mouth and screamed, "The Easter Bunny is dead!"

CHAPTER ONE

"This is all wrong." Mama scraped the side of the big pot that sat atop one of the many stoves in the Incubator, a kitchen that amateur chefs and bakers used in the back of the Freedom Diner.

"You didn't put enough water in the boiler." Nate Lustig, the diner's owner and the head honcho of the Incubator, stood over Mama's shoulder, giving her pointers. "See?" He lifted the double boiler and had Mama look inside. "All gone. Evaporated!"

He clapped, making her jump.

"We can fix it." Nate grabbed a few ingredients and some heavy cream. He poured them in while Mama vigorously stirred.

I was too busy with my own dark chocolate concoction to worry about what Mama was doing. The small bunny molds would be perfect for the dark chocolate treats I'd planned to give out to the friends I'd made in Holiday Junction while working at the Easter-egg-dyeing station for the Hip Hop Hurray Easter Festival.

It was my first Easter here, and with the huge town Bake-Off to celebrate the holiday, I'd agreed to come with Mama to the Incubator. She'd entered the Bake-Off and could perfect her Easter dirt cake here. She claimed the chocolate bunnies she was going to outline the cake with would make her the winner, which was why she insisted on getting the melted chocolate just right.

The sound of the aerosol can of cooking spray I was using to coat the bunny molds combined with the whirring of mixers and a blender, the clanging of pots and pans, the sizzling of pans on the stove, and the clinking of utensils other people used.

Nate moved around the kitchen and gave the occasional shout or conversation between himself and one of the bakers. Though this was his weekly baking class, most of the bakers in the Incubator were also contestants in the big Bake-Off.

When I heard the squeak of the oven doors opening and closing and the beeping of timers going off, I looked around to see who had either started or ended the baking process.

Frances Green had called Nate over to test the cake she'd taken out of the oven. She was one of Mama's toughest competitors.

Nate's fork slid through the slice of chocolate cake. He put it in his mouth and raked the tines along the bottoms of his teeth as a look of pure bliss forced his eyes to close.

It was almost like I could also savor the rich chocolate that made Nate's lips curl up into a satisfied smile.

"Perfect," Nate said. He let out a small sigh of contentment and then took another bite of the moist, fluffy cake.

Frances clapped in delight. The lines around her mouth deepened as her smile grew. She pushed back a few of the loose strands of grey hair that'd fallen out of her topknot and straightened her shoulders as her inner confident baker came out. It was no secret that Frances had won the Bake-Off last year and was here with a passion to win again, making the competition fierce.

Well, for Mama at least. And when I caught Mama looking at Frances, I saw a fire in Mama's eyes, one I'd seen before. The kind of spark that gave her a challenge, and that was what she lived for.

Frances reached around her waist and untied her apron before she tossed it into the dirty hamper.

"The perfect balance of sweetness and chocolate in every bite." Nate bit into the treat again as if he needed to back up his statement. "Every bite."

"Thank you." Frances slid her gaze over to Mama with a wry smile. "This isn't even the recipe I'm going to enter into the contest."

"By the smile on your face, you look like you've got someone special." Willow Johnson pulled her shoulders up to her ears as she blushed.

"I do," Frances whispered loudly enough for me to make out the words that piqued my interest. "But I can't tell anyone. Yet."

"Good for you." Willow conveyed her excitement in a touch above a hushed tone. "You deserve it. Especially after all the time you put into Holiday Junction."

I turned my body slightly so I could hear them a little better, but I wasn't quick enough.

Frances's phone alarm sounded. She took the phone out of her apron pocket.

"I'll be back later to make the one for the competition. I'm going to be late for the audition if I don't get out of here now." Frances's smile never faltered from when Willow asked about the special someone.

In fact, Frances's smile got bigger as she walked closer to Mama.

"I see you made some hollow chocolate bunnies. I bet they are so good." Frances looked over Mama's shoulder. "I love a good chocolate bunny."

Frances pointed at the ten molds Mama had made to surround her cake with the first time around.

"Would you like one?" Mama asked.

"I'd love one. Thank you, Millie Kay." Frances scanned down the line, trying to decide which bunny looked appetizing to her. "How did you know chocolate bunnies are my favorite?"

"Just a guess. I have one special just for you." Mama bent down and took one out of the baking case she'd brought from home.

"It has eyes and a little button candy nose." Frances took the one Mama had made at home for practice. Mama had even put pastel sugar candy buttons on the chocolate bunny for more detail for the nose, eyes, and teeth. "These are adorable."

"Thank you." Mama was proud of what she'd done at home, but today she couldn't even melt the chocolate properly, much less make any sort of bunnies to go around her cake.

"I'll eat this while I go judge the annual bunny competition. I can guarantee there are going to be some big changes, and some people aren't going to like them." Frances waved the chocolate bunny in the air on her way out the door. "You better hurry up."

"Mama, that was nice of you." I wanted her to know I was proud of her, since she'd been yammering on and on about Frances being tough competition for her.

"Ahem." Mama intentionally cleared her throat to make me look at her. It was her way of telling me she didn't want me to mention the kind gesture again unless it was necessary. "We'll have to come back. I have to be at the Easter Bunny auditions in about five minutes, and you have to take the photos," she said, reminding me of the article I was doing for the *Junction Journal*.

I glanced up at the clock on the wall to check the time. The past few hours had gone by fast, and I'd yet to get my mold into the refrigerator.

"Oh no," Willow Johnson cried out over the hum of her mixer. "It's already time for the audition?"

She flipped the switch and ran her fingers down the front of her apron, leaving a chocolate streak trail before she used the apron's bottom edges to wipe her hands down.

"Maximus is probably wondering where I'm at." She untied her apron, wadded it up, and placed it on the mixer. When she hurried off, it fell to the ground. "I'll be back," she called over her shoulder and ran out of the building.

"Then we have to hurry," I told her, starting to scoop my melted dark chocolate out of the pan and into the molds. "Nate," I called to him.

He looked up.

4

"Can I leave these in the freezer until later?" I asked. "We have to get to the bunny auditions."

I wasn't a judge like Mama. She was a new member on the Village Council and had the hard task of choosing the perfect bunny for the village's Hip Hop Hurray event.

"I'm going to start fresh later." Mama literally tossed everything, including the top pan of the double boiler, in the large jute sack she'd used to bring all her ingredients in from home. "Are you ready?" Mama gave me the side eye.

"Let me get these into the refrigerator and snap a few quick photos." Carefully, I picked up each mold, walked them across the test kitchen, and placed them on a shelf in the walk-in freezer.

"Violet! Let's go!" Mama had already left the Incubator and stood outside on the sidewalk, yelling for me, swinging her baking box back and forth.

"Thanks, Nate." I offered a wry smile in an attempt to apologize for Mama's behavior. At times like these, she wasn't so southern and lady-like as she thought she was.

"I think I've lost my touch," Mama whined before she picked up her speed, swinging her arms.

The weather was warm and sunny, with clear blue skies and a gentle breeze coming off the ocean. It was nice to see the beach crowded with people who had come to Holiday Junction to enjoy the holiday.

Mama stomped down the seaside sidewalk on the way toward the lighthouse. We were trying to catch the trail leading up to Holiday Park, where the main events of the Hip Hop Hurray Festival would take place.

It was best not to say anything to her or answer her when she was like this, which I'd learned a long time ago.

Instead of commenting, I grunted a few *mm-hhmm*s and did a little window shopping. It was fun to see how the small shops along the seashore had decorated their display windows. Easter-themed decorations such as bunnies, eggs, and pastel colors seemed to be the décor of choice.

A few children darted around Mama then around me as their parents called for them, but the excitement of holiday chocolate was smeared all over their faces.

I sucked in a deep breath, taking in the scent of saltwater mixed with sunscreen that filled the air. The sound of waves crashing on the shore was so soothing and made me smile.

I'd really fallen in love with Holiday Junction without even knowing it.

One big cardboard Easter Bunny was duct-taped to the black door of the jiggle joint. No doubt Darren Strickland had gone to such great efforts to fulfil the Village Council's request that all businesses in Holiday Junction put out some sort of decoration for the holiday.

It took all my willpower not to open the door and slip in where Darren Strickland was working on this week's liquor order.

"Violet Rhinehammer!" Mama stopped, turned around, threw her hands on her hips, and glared. "What are you doing? Stop lollygagging this instant," she snapped and twirled back around, walking like one of those speed walkers at the mall.

I gave one last look at the bar's door and sighed. Seeing Darren would have to wait.

"Violet!" Mama yelled her one-last-time-or-she-would-scold-me yell, even though I was almost thirty years old. "The Leisure Center will be a great place for the Leading Ladies to practice, and I found the perfect place."

"You found a place?" She got my attention, because that was a sure sign the idea had formed into a more solid planning stage.

I hurried up beside her with full attention.

"Did you hear me about the Leisure Center?" Mama had this crazy idea that Holiday Junction needed a place for seniors to go. "I'm telling you I'd be really good at helping people my age."

"Your age?" I questioned. "You're sixty."

Mama had gotten a harebrained idea that Holiday Junction needed something like a senior center, only she named it the Leisure Center.

She'd been eyeballing a few older buildings in the area, and it seemed like she'd settled on one.

"We won't have to practice outside in all the elements anymore," she said and hurried up the sidewalk leading from the seaside to Holiday Park.

The sun shone brightly on this beautiful spring day as the Hip Hop Hurray Easter Festival was being set up in the large park.

The park was bustling. Vendors were setting up their booths on the far side of the park, toward the bubbling fountain. The echo from the Leading Ladies inside the bowl of the amphitheater filled the air, as did the laughter of tourists who came off the lake as they paddled around in the large swan boats.

Spring was one of my favorite seasons, and since this was my first spring here, Holiday Junction didn't disappoint.

"I'll be over in a few!" Mama yelled at the Leading Ladies to let them know her itinerary.

Few.

"Isn't it gorgeous here?" Mama must've felt the light in her spirit too. "After a long winter, I'm so glad to have this sunshine." She tucked her arm in my elbow and pointed out what the committee had done to make this year's Hip Hop Hurray Easter Festival the best yet.

And that included her participation in the Leading Ladies production as well as taking home the Golden Egg Trophy for winning the stiff baking competition.

The park was adorned with colorful decorations and flowers hanging from baskets suspended from the planters on the carriage lights. The banners hanging from the dowel rods fluttered in the breeze, adding to the festive atmosphere. The large fountain in the park's center was a popular spot, with children running around and splashing in the cool water.

It was funny to see seven Easter Bunnies all lined up near a banquet table in various types of outfits, trying to win the coveted title to play the Easter Bunny during the entire Hip Hop Hurray Easter Festival. They took that very seriously around here.

"Don't forget to get me sitting at the judges' table," Mama told me as she ran her hand over her shoulder-length blond hair with a hint of gray around the scalp. Her makeup was as perfect as if she'd just left the makeup counter at a high-end department store.

Mama was every part of the southern lady she had always been, even though we no longer lived in the South.

"How do I look?" She tugged at the hem of her monogrammed three-quarter-length sweater as it lay against her jeans.

"You look fantastic," I told her. "And you'll be the prettiest picture I take all day."

Mama hurried over to the judges' table and sat in the chair on the far right, leaving a chair open between her and Emily, the owner of Emily's Treasures. Frances hadn't taken her middle seat at the judges' table. I took the moment to snap a few shots of Mama sitting there so Frances wouldn't be in the photos. Or at least I wouldn't have to crop them out if Mama was standing over my shoulder at the office while I wrote the article.

I moseyed around, slipping in and out of the crowd milling around the park to get some action shots for the *Junction Journal*.

There were six bunnies in costume, and they were all completely different. They were also carrying baskets filled to the brim with colored eggs. Some looked to be the real dyed kind, making me shiver, since I'd done my civic duty as a member of the village and volunteered for a couple of hours during the festival at the egg-dyeing table. The other baskets looked like they were filled with plastic eggs. But the one bunny basket that really got my attention was the one with the two little baby bunnies nestled inside.

"Easter Bunny," I said as I approached and wiggled my camera in the air, "may I take your photo for the *Junction Journal*?"

The bunny nodded and then turned slightly, gave the little cotton tail a little wiggle, and came my way with a little hopping action.

Before too long, the four other bunnies had hopped over, trying to get me to take a photo.

They had really gotten their ability to grab a child's attention down—and my attention too.

One hopped around in a playful manner, attempting to catch my eye by playing peek-a-boo. Another had started to clap the paws and give a little squeal while waving at me.

But the one who rattled a plastic egg, indicating that something was inside, and then offered it to me really got my attention.

"I'm a sucker for Easter candy," I teased and snapped a few photos that included all the bunnies before they hopped away.

I sure didn't envy Mama, Emily, and Frances's job. They were going to have a hard time picking which one would be the best because they all looked great to me.

All but the fifth one, who wore a distinctive bow tie and had not tried to come over but was hopping toward the judges' table.

"Smart," I whispered and brought the camera up to my eye, using my hand to manually zoom in.

In the bliss of watching the bunny stand behind Mama and tease her by trying to take her baking box, I didn't even see Darren Strickland come up behind me.

"Looks like someone is trying to win over Millie Kay." His deep voice and warm breath on my ear made me jump.

"You scared me, Darren Strickland." I playfully smacked him on the arm. "I see the Mad Fiddlers are setting up after the Leading Ladies rehearse."

"I think the Merry Maker picked an *egg*-cellent spot this year." Darren made a horrible joke.

As the editor, photographer, journalist and pretty much the only employee at the *Junction Journal*, even though Mama had recently joined on as part of my research team, I had all the schedules for the holiday functions so I could take photos and report on them.

And because I was Holiday Junction's secret Merry Maker, it was nice to be able to have the inside scoop publicly, making the secret job much easier to perform.

The rules about the Merry Maker weren't clear. The only rules were these: no one could know, and a person-sized sign in the shape of the holiday had to be planted in the area where the Merry Maker wanted the holiday's last hurrah to take place. No one had ever known if co-Merry Makers existed, but I decided on that rule when Darren caused Mama to find out about my secret identity.

"Yes, they did." I stared into his dark eyes, resisting the urge to curl up on my tiptoes and kiss him. Instead, I reached up and mussed the longer curls in his dark hair.

"Stop." He batted me away. "Seriously. Do you like it?"

"I love it." I twisted my shoulders toward the amphitheater. A huge wooden cutout of a decorated Easter egg was placed near it. "It's a perfect place to end the festival. And the Mad Fiddlers are playing too."

I hadn't picked the amphitheater as the final hurrah for the festival because Darren's band was playing—not that I didn't choose that spot for that reason. Even though Darren and I had become co-Merry Makers, which I suspected was a first after hundreds of years, and I was wildly attracted to him, I wanted his band to be popular. If I had the power to let them be part of the final Easter celebration, I was going to do that.

"Thank you," he said, his eyes softening under his thick dark brows. "I know you suggested it for me."

He leaned in just enough to get my heart racing and my mind believing he was about to kiss me. Right there. In front of everyone.

A bloodcurdling scream made us jerk apart and look to see who was in desperate need of help.

The six Easter Bunnies scattered in different directions. Make that seven, because the one Mama was standing over lay flat on his fluffy back. Colorfully decorated Easter eggs had spilled out of the white basket and were strewn all around the costumed person auditioning for the part.

Mama brought her hands over her mouth and screamed, "The Easter Bunny is dead!"

CHAPTER TWO

"Oh my stars, oh my stars." Mama couldn't stop saying it as she fiddled with the strand of pearls that lay perfectly on her collarbone. "What on earth do you think happened to her?"

"Mama." I grabbed her by the shoulders and tried not to look at the surprise underneath after Chief Matthew Strickland showed up and unmasked the bunny. "Let Matthew do his job."

I tried not to stare into Frances Green's open eyes. The sparkling bright eyes she'd had in the Incubator, showing the pride in how her cake had turned out, were now just dark abysses.

"What is this?" one of the sheriff's deputies asked Matthew, pointing at Frances's fist.

"It looks like some sort of chocolate something or other." Matthew had bent down to see what the deputy was pointing at.

"It's a chocolate bunny," Mama cried. "At least she got to taste my bunny before she died." Mama hung her head.

Matthew whispered something into the deputy's ear before he rushed over and pushed the gathering crowd back from the scene.

"What are they doing?" Mama asked, trying to aim her gaze over my shoulders as I moved them so she couldn't see. "Violet Rhinehammer, stop moving around."

"Mama, you don't need to see this." Nobody needed to see this, but at least in my line of work, I'd seen many dead bodies. The sight never got any easier to stomach, though. "Why don't you go on over to the amphitheater with the other Leading Ladies while they sort this out?"

Mama gave a couple of quick nods and twisted around. She took the shortcut across the grass to get there.

"Did you see that?" I asked Darren. I couldn't help but notice the deputy had taken an evidence baggy and put the half-eaten chocolate bunny in it.

"I did." He glanced down at me with a look of deep thought that I'd seen before. "And I know what it means if Dad takes this much time to get a dead person to the morgue."

Just as Darren said that, Curtis Robinson, the coroner, whipped past us, carrying his medical examiner bag. You didn't see that bag unless there was a reason to believe the death was suspect.

Four of the bunnies had their costume heads off and tucked up under their arms. Their hair was matted to their foreheads from the sticky sweat that formed underneath the costume heads. The only bunny I recognized was Owen, a regular at the jiggle joint.

"Where are the other two bunnies?" I asked Darren.

"One is on the ground." He pointed out the obvious.

"No. There were seven bunnies." I pointed and counted out loud. "One, two, three, four, and Frances makes five. But where are the other two?"

"Are you sure there were seven including Frances?" he asked.

"Yes." I nodded and shifted my gaze back to Frances's body but looked more closely at Matthew.

I'd worked with Matthew before on an investigation, and I knew the way he conducted a murder scene. This situation appeared to be just that.

A homicide.

He had the deputies move back the crowd, and then he enclosed some things in evidence bags and called the coroner in.

After any death, the coroner typically came and made sure the person had, in fact, died. The coroner also called a time of death, but when Curtis came with his little black bag, which contained all sorts of equipment that was needed to carefully take samples of things, I knew this death was being treated as a homicide.

I watched as Matthew appeared to look around for something. Like he needed something. I saw him whisper something to Curtis before he started across the grass toward the crowd.

I should've kept my eye on Matthew to see where he was going, but he wasn't the one who caught my attention. Curtis Robinson was.

He knelt next to Frances. He put one hand on her bunny arm and used his other hand to cover his eyes. He was visibly upset, but he tried very hard to cover it.

Matthew got in the way of my view. I sidestepped to the right to look around him. Curtis had shifted his position and opened the medical bag so he could prepare to do the initial assessment of Frances's body and then move her onto the gurney that would eventually transport her back to the morgue.

Matthew stopped shy of the crowd and scanned, looking directly at me before he stepped over to us.

"Can you run over to the department and grab me something to use for crime scene tape?" he asked Darren. "It seems like we are out."

"Out of Do Not Cross tape?" I questioned.

"Yes. It would seem very strange, I know, but in light of the recent homicides, it appears that we've used up all we had, and we've not had to order any in, well, over ten years." His brows hooded his eyes as he stared at me and directed his words at me, as if these murders were my fault.

"There's extra crepe paper over on the judges' table," I suggested.

"The pink and green streamers?" Matthew asked.

"That's a great idea. You can use those until you can find something to put up in their place." Darren told him in no uncertain terms he wouldn't go back to the department to find something his dad could use.

"Fine." Matthew didn't look fine as he stalked away to retrieve the crepe paper from the judges' table.

In a few minutes, the deputy had used the pink and green streamers to rope off the area from the rest of the park, making the area look more like a decoration than a crime scene.

"Why don't you take your mama on back to the office while I continue to see what's going on here?" Darren didn't have to tell me that he was thinking the same thing I was—that Mama looked like a suspect.

"Are you sure?" I asked when I saw Curtis stand up and glance toward the amphitheater, where Mama was being consoled by Louise Strickland, fellow Leading Lady, Matthew's wife, and our boss at the *Junction Journal*.

Yeah. Things could get really sticky, since Holiday Junction was so small that practically everyone was related to everyone else somehow, even if it was very distant.

"Yeah. The time is now, and you might want to call Diffy Delk." He suggested something I'd already thought of. And Diffy was the only lawyer in town, so there weren't many options.

"I was thinking the same thing." I put my hand on Darren's forearm. "Let me know if you hear anything."

"I will." He gestured for me to go.

I wasn't sure if I was able to leave the scene, since Frances's death didn't appear to be due to a heart attack or some other natural cause. However, they'd not yet told us to stay put, which was something Matthew did so he could interview everyone who was present during past homicide investigations.

He'd ask certain kinds of questions to see if anyone saw or heard anything unusual.

"Louise, Marge." I gave my two bosses a solid nod. "Mama, let's go back to the office so we can get some of the Hip Hop Hurray photos up while they do their thing."

"That's a great idea. I'm sure people will be going straight to the online paper after news of Frances's passing gets around town." Louise was dressed in a long caftan and matching headscarf.

"Good thinking," Marge agreed, her sleek silver hair moving as she nodded. "After all, the *Junction Journal* isn't out of the woods yet." Darren's aunt was good at reminding me that the newspaper was on the brink of extinction before I took their job offer to run it.

I wasn't planning on staying after a dead body was found on the flight out to California, where I was interviewing for my dream job at a big-time newspaper. The pilot made an emergency landing, and guess where that was?

Mm-hhmm, the small town of Holiday Junction.

As luck, or just my luck would have it, the dead passenger, like Frances, didn't die of natural causes, and Matthew wasn't about to let any airplane take off until the murder was solved.

Of course I used my amazing journalism skills and keen ear for listening to clues to help Matthew solve the murder so I could get on with my upcoming career. The two sisters-in-law, however, gave me an offer I couldn't refuse.

I mean, I literally couldn't refuse because I never made it to the interview that day in California, and someone else got the job. That left me homeless and penniless, so any job would've been better than none.

I had no clue how much the newspaper was in trouble. They didn't even have an office or an online edition. Establishing both of those was my first duty as the new editor in chief and really the only employee.

"I'll take Mama with me. She can help do some research about the history of the Easter festival so I get all the facts straight." I tugged on Mama's sleeve.

"I think I'll just stay here. Maybe take a sick day because I'm not feeling so well." Mama would have to be told to come, or they'd haul her off to the police station, and she would really be sick. I had a deep-rooted feeling that was where this was going.

"Mama, I need your help." It was one of those statements I knew I would regret as soon as it passed my perfectly lined red lips, which was also because of Mama.

I could never leave the house without lipstick on when I was growing up, and it was a daily reminder now, even though I was almost thirty.

"You do?" She gasped about as much as she did when she saw Frances was lying on the ground, dressed in the bunny suit.

"I do." I tucked my hand in the crook of her elbow and twisted her toward the path, leading us back down to the seaside so we could get out of there as quickly as possible. "Now while I upload the photos in the computer, I want you to…"

I stopped talking once I knew we were out of earshot of the Stricklands and out of sight of Holiday Park.

"Mama…" I sucked in a deep breath before I said what I was about to say. "I think Frances was murdered."

"Murdered!" she yelped, startling the tourists walking along the ocean's sidewalk. "By who?"

"I don't know who, but I think they think it's you." I knew the words were going to sting.

"Me? Why on earth me?" A look of fear I'd never seen before in Mama's eyes was almost as painful to see as the sad eyes I'd only observed from her once, when her mother died.

"It looks like she was eating the bunny you gave her." I was going to tell her that I noticed the bunny was bagged up, but she interrupted me.

"How do they know that was my bunny?" Mama picked up her speed a smidgen as we hurried past all the quaint seaside shops and the small one-street neighborhood. Then we took the path from the sea through the landscape and roped-off turtle nest to the cottage that served as the Junction Journal office.

"Did you give her one of your chocolate bunnies from the Incubator?" I asked, even though I'd seen her do it. I unlocked the office door and pushed it open for her to enter ahead of me.

"I did, but she had to have eaten that already. Besides, they can test my bunnies." She stopped shy of the threshold. "My baking box…"

She swiveled her body around.

"I've got to go back and get it." She took a step back toward the sea.

"No, Mama, you can't. Leave it," I told her. "I need to call Diffy Delk."

"Why on earth would you do such a thing?" Mama shoved her fisted hands on her hips and eyeballed me.

"Because of that—" I barely got the words out as my mouth dried, and I pointed with a shaky finger when Chief Strickland's police cruiser pulled into the office's small driveway.

CHAPTER THREE

"You mean to tell me your mother has been arrested for murder again?" Diffy Delk sat behind the large oak desk that was too big for his office.

He held out a piece of his chocolate bunny, and Dave the Rooster took it.

"I'm not so sure that's good for roosters." The words left my mouth before I could reel them back in. "I mean, I know it's not good for house pets. And Dave is a very important part of our community," I stammered, trying to find the words.

"This isn't real chocolate." Diffy's brows rose high on his elongated forehead, almost touching the edges of his toupee. "You're right." He ran his finger down one of the rooster's feathers. "He is the best security guard we've got around here."

Dave was almost as popular as Holiday Junction's Mayor Paisley, who just so happened to be a Boston terrier, as in the dog.

Treating Paisley as the mayor was a tradition for the village to raise money, since the village was really run by a council. But in Dave the Rooster's case, well, I had no idea how it came to be that he was an outstanding security guard at the Holiday Junction airport.

Since the airport was so small—it had only one room—it was open just once a week. That was for one flight, incoming and outgoing. Granted, if someone needed to get on an airplane, they could drive for about an hour to a bigger city with a regular-size airport.

Since today was not the flying day, Dave was here with Diffy, his owner.

"Again," I grumbled under my breath, realizing this was the second time Mama had been accused of killing someone. "Yes. I think again."

"Either she has or she hasn't." Diffy sat up on the edge of his office chair. The sleeves of his brown polyester suit dragged up past his wrists, and the edges of his burnt-yellow long-sleeved silk shirt peeked out as he rested his arms atop his desk with his hands folded.

He wore a gold square ring on his finger and a tarnished gold watch on his wrist.

"Can you do what you did last time?" I pulled out a white envelope from my purse and set it on top of the desk in clear view of his hungry eyes. "Your retainer is all here."

He reached across and raked the envelope across the desk, peeking inside and counting the hundred-dollar bills as he dragged his thumb through them.

"Your motto is 'I fought the law and I won,'" I said, reminding him about the words he so proudly flashed on his website.

He opened the top desk drawer and slipped the envelope inside.

"Start from the beginning." Diffy picked up an ink pen and grabbed a legal-size pad of paper.

He scribbled while I told him what had happened.

"It wasn't until I noticed the deputy had bagged up the chocolate bunny that I even thought Frances had been murdered," I said, watching him take the chocolate bunny he was gnawing on with Dave and put it in the trash can next to the desk.

"How do you know it was one of the bunnies Millie Kay made at home?" He could tell the ones she'd made at home from the ones she'd ruined at the Incubator because I'd told him the story.

"The ones she made at home were in her baking box. She'd decorated them with candy dots. The eyes, nose, you know," I said.

"Why do you think Frances was poisoned?" he asked. When I'd described how Frances looked lying on the ground, I mentioned poison. "And why do you think it was Millie Kay's bunny?"

"Mama gave her one of the bunnies from her baking box when Frances was leaving the Incubator. She was grasping it when she died. After Curtis showed up, he pretty much seemed to think Frances was poisoned. At least that was according to Matthew when he showed up at the office to take Mama down for questioning."

Diffy smacked the desk with a flat hand.

Dave the Rooster jerked to life. His wings spread out, and he fluttered off the desk.

"Questioning." Diffy lifted his finger in the air. "They have no idea if the bunny Frances was eating was the one Millie Kay had given her." He leaned over his desk, looked into the trash, and picked out the bunny he'd thrown away. "I'm alive."

He waved the bunny in the air.

"Is that one of Mama's bunnies?" I asked.

"It is. I saw her on the trolley this morning. She was going to the office, and she gave a bunny or two to Goldie Bennett to put in her grandkids' baskets. Now, I don't think Millie Kay is going around trying to poison all the people in town. That leads me to believe something or someone else killed Frances." His voice drifted off, as did his faraway look. "But who, Violet? That's the question."

"So you think they have no evidence to hold Mama?" I asked to make sure I understood what Diffy was saying.

Did anyone ever really understand him?

"They do not, unless they can determine if the chocolate bunny in Frances's grip was, in fact, poisoned and came from Millie Kay's kitchen. Then we have a problem." He stood up, and I followed him. "Until then, we will go right over there and see what they have on the case. Maybe they are just taking her in for questioning, since she was a judge. You know, try to see if she noticed anything."

He walked past me and held the office door for me.

"The Easter Bunny auditions here are stiff competition." He didn't need to tell me how whack-a-doodle people around here were about every holiday, not just Easter.

"Anything new?" I asked Darren, who we found waiting outside of Diffy's office.

"No. I tried to get answers out of my dad, but you know him. All tight-lipped." Darren's jaw set. "Diffy, you think you can work some Diffy Delk magic?"

"Is my name Diffy Delk?" Diffy Delk drew his shoulders back. I wasn't so sure whether that statement gave me comfort or not, but there was no other choice.

He led the way out of the building and just across the street to the police station, Darren and I following closely behind him.

Diffy stood like a statue as his eyes scanned the police department until they settled on Matthew's office. The shades on that office's glass wall were slightly closed but open enough for me to see Mama in there talking to Matthew and another deputy.

"You can't go in there, Mr. Delk." A woman tried to stop him as he bolted through the door.

"Chief, do you have reasonable cause to hold my client?" Diffy asked. Then he instructed Mama, "Don't say a word."

"She's said plenty of words." Matthew gazed past Darren and held my stare for a brief moment before he moved to look at Darren. "And the preliminary test on the chocolate bunny shows large amounts of temazepam."

"The sleep aid?" I asked, since I'd done a lot of research while writing various articles over the year.

"Yes." Matthew wasn't about to give more details than necessary. "We've sent an officer over to your parents' house because Millie Kay confessed to getting the doctor here to prescribe her the sleep aid, since she hadn't been getting much sleep."

My eyes grew when I looked at Mama.

"This is the first I'm hearing this." Mama told me everything. I mean everything, including some things I didn't want to know. Especially when it came to her and my daddy having marital issues.

She had no filter or boundaries when it came to anything.

"We also have deputies over there with a search warrant." Matthew looked at Diffy so Diffy didn't ask if they'd gotten the proper paperwork. "It does appear she'll be staying for a few days."

"Diffy, you get me out of here right now. This instant!" Mama thrust her finger down to the floor and stamped her foot. "This is ridiculous. And you." Mama moved that finger and jutted it at Matthew. "You oughta be ashamed of yourself, hauling a lady down here like this. Acting as though I was some murderous criminal when I'm the mama of the Mer…"

"Mama." I stopped her before she told the secret about me being the Merry Maker. "There's no reason for you to get your blood pressure up. Let Diffy sort things out with the authorities."

I gave Matthew a hard look.

"Then we will get you home soon." I patted her on the shoulder. "If you don't mind doing your job and bringing her back to the office, I'd kindly appreciate it."

"She's in good hands," Darren told me. He put his hand on me, indicating that he wanted me to leave. "Let's let Diffy do his job." Even though I'd told Diffy to bring her back to the office, I'd really said it for Mama's sake so she could feel as if she were going to get out soon.

But it took Darren's assurance to physically get me to move.

"Don't worry, Mama." I bent down and kissed her on the head. At no time did I appreciate Mama's Chanel No. 5 perfume more than this moment.

As strange as it sounded and as much as that scent drove me crazy when I could smell her before seeing her coming, there was a comfort in it. A realization she was always there for me.

When I decided to make a life in Holiday Junction, who showed up on my doorstep? Mama.

And she wasn't alone. She'd brought her suitcases and eventually Daddy and their entire life so we could all be together.

That was Mama.

A southern mama who'd do anything to make sure I was healthy and happy.

Now it was my turn to once again get Mama out of a pickle.

CHAPTER FOUR

"What are you doing?" Darren sighed, folded his arms, and leaned his shoulder up against the threshold of my office door.

"I thought I asked you to put on a pot of coffee when you offered to help." With a shaky hand, I ran the dry eraser across the scheduled events for the Hip Hop Hurray Festival. I needed to start writing down all the information I needed to look at a clear picture of who killed Frances and why they would kill her.

"By the erratic behavior you're showing, I think coffee is the last thing you need." Did Darren really think he knew what was best for me?

"Then you can leave." Using my teeth, I pulled the cap off the dry-erase marker and wrote Frances Green's name with a few bullet points underneath.

"I don't want to leave. I want to stay here with you." He pushed his shoulder off the doorjamb and stood up tall.

"Did you ask me on the way here how you could help me?" With the tip of the marker on the first bullet point, I looked over my shoulder at him. "I want a coffee. So you can either make a pot or go get me one from Brewing Beans."

"I can see you're not going to budge." He turned to leave through the door but stopped and turned back. "Check your camera. You might see something in the photos." He walked down the small hallway to go to the cottage's kitchen.

"That's a great idea." I would've remembered the photos I'd taken eventually and was a little disappointed in myself that I'd not thought of them sooner. This only told me I was running on stress and frantically trying to help Mama when I needed to use my journalistic mind to get some truly solid motives and suspects.

Next to each bullet point underneath Frances's name, I quickly wrote one or two words exploring why there might be motive.

Next to bullet point one, I wrote "Bake-Off championship."

Beside bullet point two, I wrote "bunny competition."

For bullet point three, I wrote "public fights or arguments."

All of those seemed to be activities Frances had been involved in recently, and any of them could have been a reason to, well, let her expire.

The smell of coffee wafted down the hall. I sucked in a deep breath through my nose and let the aroma slowly travel to my foggy brain. The sheer smell of caffeine gave my mind a little jolt to wake up.

I popped the lid back on the marker and put it on the desk so I could retrieve my camera.

"I think I've got some good reasons," I said when I heard Darren's footsteps approaching.

I popped the digital card out and slipped it into the side of my laptop.

"It'll be ready in a few." Darren came back into the office. He looked at the board and crossed his arms, rocking back on the heels of his shoes.

While I waited for the photos to upload and pop up on the screen, I looked at Darren. He seemed to be pondering the bullet points a little more than I'd anticipated.

"Since you are from here, you might know something from a long time ago that had to do with Frances." I turned back to the computer.

One by one, the photos I'd taken layered on top of one another, with so many pops of bright colors, smiling faces, and fully costumed bunny rabbits who had no idea one of them would soon be targeted.

"One of them." My jaw dropped. I grabbed the marker, removed the cap, and returned to the white board. Next to Frances's name, I wrote down the question in my head. "Why was Frances in a bunny costume?" I said each word as I wrote it.

"Good question. But I was thinking about what you said about seven bunnies." He reignited the thought I'd had forgotten about when it all first happened. "Can you distinguish seven different bunny costumes on here?"

"I remember thinking that each one was different." I sat down at my desk chair and brought the mouse to life so I could use it to drag the photos along the desktop and look at them collectively. "This one has a polka-dot bow tie, while this one has a red mouth, and this one has purple silk on the inside of the bunny ears."

"This one has a folded ear." Darren caught one I'd not seen. "That's four. I guess we can count out the one Frances was wearing."

"She had really long eyelashes, like a girl bunny." Wow, I shocked myself, since I'd not thought I'd really remembered anything after Mama had started screaming. "That's five. Now where are the other two?"

My eyes scanned the photos. I minimized a few so I could enlarge different ones.

"There." Darren pointed at one of the photos I'd taken of Mama sitting at the judges' table when I took advantage of Frances's absence so I didn't have to crop her out. "There's the bunny toe."

The mouse clicked a few times while I used it to enlarge the photo.

"And if you look closely at the table, it looks like it's the score sheets." I twisted around to the whiteboard and looked at the second bullet point. "So we might have a bunny killer who saw the sheet and wasn't ranking so well."

"It's a shot at a motive at least." Darren didn't bother asking if he should write it on the board. I was happy to think he was there to really help as he took the initiative to write down "bunny toes in photo exhibit A."

"Exhibit A?" I laughed.

"What?" he asked nonchalantly. "Print out the photo, and we will tape it up like those crime shows do."

He made the best suggestion, and I let the copier whirl. Eventually, it spat out all the photos.

"How would Millie Kay have motive to kill Frances over the bunny competition?"

We both clearly wanted to point the suspect finger at someone and find reasons why Mama wouldn't have a motive.

"None, unless you consider that Mama was put on the judges' panel because of her newest position on the village council." Both of us stopped to think for a moment. "Unless someone on the council has something against Frances and made Mama a convenient target, since Frances and Mama did have competition in the baking department."

"What about the baking competition?" He pointed at the bullet point then wrote down a note to see what village council members had a beef with Frances.

He took the photo of Mama sitting at the judges' table, which also included the bunny toe, and cut off a piece of Scotch tape to post it up on the board. Next to it, he wrote Mama's name.

"Frances has been the winner for years from what I understand. She and Mama were both at the Incubator a lot over the last few weeks. Mama made it known a few times that she had to beat Frances to win." I chewed on my lip because I didn't want to say what I was about to. "Mama was frustrated today right before she and Frances needed to leave the Incubator to go judge the bunny competition, and, well…" I sucked in a deep breath and just blurted it out. "Mama gave Frances a bunny with all the candy buttons on it, one she'd made at home. The same one in her hand found at the scene."

"Oh." Darren's forehead wrinkled, and his cheeks balled as the information fell on him as if he realized the severity of what I'd just said did make Mama a real suspect. "That's not a big deal."

"Not a big deal?" I scoffed and watched as he wrote that down on the white board.

It took everything I had not to rip the marker out of his hand and use the fatty side of my hand to quickly erase it.

"I have photos to go along with the Incubator too." Instead of letting the anxiety of the situation get to me, I had to focus on how I knew Mama didn't poison Frances—at least on purpose. "If Frances was poisoned, Diffy Delk was poisoned."

"What?" Darren jerked back.

I told him that the chocolate bunny Diffy had been eating when I went to hire him for Mama was from the same baking box, which also meant it was from the same recipe batch she had given to Frances.

"When I told Diffy about Mama and the bunnies, he stopped eating it and threw it in the trash."

"We need to get that bunny from the trash." Darren quickly thumbed through the photos I'd just printed from this morning's Incubator lesson.

"But also this morning, Nate Lustig couldn't stop raving about Frances's cake." I frowned. "Mama's cake and bunnies were a flop. Like, a big flop."

"Being competitive is Millie Kay's downfall." He wrote the word "competition" next to Mama's name. "But that doesn't make her a killer."

I looked back over at the whiteboard, which truly was starting to look like the kind I'd seen on several television shows.

"Bunny competition. Baking competition. Public fight." Out loud, I read off the three main bullet points we'd come up with.

"Since we don't have clear motives for all of these, I think our first stop should be visiting village council members." I used the marker to circle the notes Darren had jotted down under Mama's name, which was listed as the suspect.

Mama was always cracking up at the public arguments that happened in the weekly village council meetings. Frances Green was vocal. If she was this vocal about a little bunny competition or even a baking competition, she could be passionate about so many more things during a village council meeting. It was up to me to thumb through those meeting notes to see what got Frances lit up.

"Are you okay? You look a little peaked," Darren said, bringing me out of my thoughts.

"I'm fine." I couldn't stop myself from staring at Mama's name and her happy photo, in which she was so excited to be sitting at the judges' table. "She was so happy. I just know she had no notion in her noggin to do such a horrible thing."

"We have good ideas on where to start while Diffy works on getting her out of the police station." Darren made me feel so much better.

"What do you say we ditch the coffeepot here and grab some from Brewing Beans along with some sweets for Mayor Paisley?" I asked Darren.

"I'm right behind you," he said. He must have wanted to get in front of Kristine Whitlock, since we knew that she went to the village council meetings because Mayor Paisley went. And Kristine always had her ear on the pulse of the gossip in Holiday Junction. I was positive we'd be able to sort through it to find Frances Green's real killer.

CHAPTER FIVE

With so many questions left unanswered, it felt good to get some of my nervous energy out by getting out of the office and away from all the lingering what-if scenarios. We could at least check one of them off the list.

It was time to see if any of the village council members had a personal enough vendetta against Frances to get her kicked off the council... permanently.

The ding of the trolley echoed around the shoreline before we'd seen Goldie Bennett driving toward us. I couldn't make out Goldie's face, but I could definitely see the outline of a bunny-eared headband on top of her head.

"Where do you need a hop and a skip to?" Goldie asked as she shoved the lever, opening the door.

"Brewing Beans." Darren put his hand on the folding trolley door and used the other to gesture for me to go first.

After I'd made the couple of steps up into the trolley, I took a seat right behind Goldie, who winked and whispered, "He's such a gentleman." I recalled Diffy mentioning that he'd seen Mama on the trolley.

"He is." I nodded and scooted up to the edge of the bench seat and held on to the bar. "Mama took the trolley to the Incubator this morning, right?"

"Millie Kay sure did, and she had everyone in here salivating over them chocolate bunnies too." Goldie watched for Darren to sit down before she shoved the door closed and took off down the street along the shoreline, where she turned the trolley around to head the long way to town. "I'm so grateful she gave me those bunnies for little Lizzie, Joey, and Chance."

Goldie loved to talk about her grandchildren. I would've asked her about them if I hadn't needed to know this information about Mama.

"Do you happen to still have those bunnies?" Darren asked.

"Yes. I've got them all tucked away so no one will steal them." She had her hands curled around the large trolley steering wheel at the ten o'clock and two o'clock positions. Every once in a while, she gave Darren and me a stray look, but for the most part, she kept her eyes on the road.

I scooted to the edge of the seat and leaned over very far, catching myself from falling over into the aisle.

"Are you okay?" Goldie jerked over her right arm and looked at me.

"I'm going to need you to give the chocolate bunnies back to me," I whispered.

"Why on earth would I do that?" she snapped in an even louder tone than I'd anticipated. "No one has them. They sold out in hours at the Bubbly Boutique, Brewing Beans, and Jovial General Store." She rattled off the names of local businesses that would've kept the Easter treats in stock.

"I'm guessing you've not heard about—" I was about to say "Frances Green," but she beat me to the punch.

"Frances Green and your mama's bunny being the murderer." I didn't know why I found it funny when she said "your mama's bunny being the murderer," but I looked silly laughing out loud when my mama was still in jail for a murder I was sure she hadn't committed.

I flung my long blond hair behind my back along with my head and burst out laughing.

"I think she's lost her mind." Darren patted me on the back with a look of horror on his face as he tried to explain the situation to all the other passengers on the trolley, who visibly shifted in their seats away from us.

Away from me.

"Why didn't I think of this?" I smacked my palms on my knees. "Someone poisoned Mama's bunny at the Incubator."

"We did kinda talk about the baking competition." Darren reminded me of the bullet points we'd made on the board at the *Junction Journal* office.

"No." I shook my head. "Someone poisoned Mama's bunny this morning at the Incubator, and that was what killed Frances."

"I'm not following you." Darren eased back in the seat, giving me his full attention. He was trying to figure out what I was saying.

"Mama had given away at least four of the bunnies we know of so far. I'm not sure how many she made, but we know for a fact Diffy Delk isn't dead, and really, without testing the ones we know are out there, including Goldie's three grandchildren's, we can assume the entire batch wasn't poisoned." I knew it all sounded jumbled up when it came out of my mouth, but in my head, it sounded perfectly fine.

"When Millie Kay was at the Incubator, someone took her bunny out of the baking box and poisoned it because they knew she was going to give it to Frances?" Well, Darren had me there.

"I'm not sure, but I do know that we need to get the bunny from Diffy Delk's trash can and those three of Goldie's—or just traces of them—tested for poisoning. And we need the initial autopsy of Frances's body." This scenario had so many moving parts. By the look on Darren's face, his head was already swimming with confusion, and I'd not yet really gotten started. "Keep up," I teased and sat back in the seat. "Goldie, take us to the trolley stop in the business district."

"Okay." She sighed, and with one hand on the wheel and her eyes on the road, she bent over to the left, retrieved the three plastic-wrapped chocolate bunnies Mama had made, and handed them back to me.

"Little Lizzie sure is going to be disappointed when her basket from me doesn't have a chocolate bunny in it."

"I'm sure the Easter Bunny will give her one." I hoped to make her feel better.

"Speaking of the Easter Bunny..." Goldie whipped the trolley around the back roads from the seaside through the wooded area of Holiday Junction. Then we made a sharp right on the main street, where we passed the fancy houses, including the Strickland compound. "Did Owen final in the competition?"

"Owen, the Easter Bunny," I snickered because he always introduced himself to the bar's patrons as the Easter Bunny, but I never really figured he would act on his words. "What did he say about the competition?" I turned the question to Darren.

"I didn't even think about asking him what was going on behind the scene of the auditions." Darren's thick brows dipped. "It looks like we will be talking to him tonight. Are you free for dinner?"

"Dinner? You serve real food at the jiggle joint now?" I asked.

"No, but I hear Carnevale is really decorated for Easter." His eyes softened. "I thought we could get some good pasta for our brains."

"I thought carbs made you fall asleep," Goldie interjected. "He's asking you out on a real date, not those late-night rendezvous you two have that you think no one knows about."

"We are not having night rendezvous," I blurted out. "Not like you think, anyway." I clamped my mouth shut for fear of saying too much.

Yes. There was a spark between Darren and me. Yes. We'd kissed a couple of times. Yes. We seemed to enjoy each other's company. Date? He'd never asked me out on a date.

"Thank you for clarifying that for me, Goldie." Darren sucked in a deep breath and turned back to me. "Would you like to go out on a date with me tonight?"

"I'd love to." I tried not to smile, but my inner little girl couldn't stop the excitement growing. "I'd love to," I said again and nodded with a huge grin.

"I think he heard you the first time." Goldie brought the trolley to a stop. "Business district!" she yelled and turned over her right shoulder to stare at us.

"Thank you for giving these back. I promise I'll have Mama make you more when she can." I knew time was limited between now and Easter, but I was willing to make chocolate bunnies if I had to. "Even if I have to make them."

"Just as long as you get me three, I'm good." Goldie kept her hand on the lever at all times when operating the door. "Have a hoppy day!" she called out as soon as we stepped off the trolley. She shook her head so the bunny ears wiggled around.

Darren and I were eerily silent on the way into Diffy Delk's office, where we had to retrieve the half-eaten Easter bunny from his trash can. It was as if the dynamics between us had changed now that he'd asked me out on an official date.

Sure, we'd had a couple of beers while sitting on top of the light-house where he lived, and that was really cool. We'd also gotten a few burgers and to-go plates from Freedom Diner. Many times we'd gotten a coffee from Brewing Beans, but we had never made plans to go to a sit-down restaurant.

"So, you're going to pick me up?" I asked, wondering if he would use his moped.

Yes. The thirty-year-old man drove a moped, but half the village did unless they had golf carts, since it was kind of ridiculous to own a car in Holiday Junction. The village was compact with everything in walking distance. But some people did own cars.

"I'll figure it out. You just have to worry about being ready when I get there." He playfully nudged me. "This isn't going to be weird, is it?" He held the office door open and wiggled a finger between him and me.

"Not at all. I think it's going to be nice to actually sit down and talk." Darren and I had danced around our feelings about one another. We'd flirted and kissed, but we'd never really got down to seeing if this was really going to go somewhere.

"We should put the rumors to rest." Darren was referring to what Goldie had mentioned about us sneaking around at all hours of the night, which was true, but only because we were trying to do the co-Merry Maker job. Even then, it was only during the holidays.

Around here, it seemed like people celebrated a holiday every time the clock struck midnight.

"You first." He'd put an end to the discussion and ushered me into Diffy's office.

"He was eating the bunny as I told him about Mama's misfortunes." I didn't call it hauling her down to the station, because it was a misfortune, and I didn't want to even think about it. "It was like he feared being poisoned."

In my head, I relived Diffy taking the bite and then throwing the chocolate bunny in the trash as I told him what happened to Frances.

"He threw it in here." I picked up the trash can and turned it over. "Nothing."

"Are you sure it was that trash can?" Darren asked and walked around the small office space, looking down at the floor. "Maybe there's another one."

"No, it was this one." I was certain, and I heard some squeaking outside of the office.

I hurried over to the door and stuck my head out just in time to see the janitor push the cleaning cart around the corner of the hallway.

"Janitor!" I jerked to stand and took off down the hall toward the building employee. "Excuse me!" I called after her. "Did you clean Diffy Delk's office space?"

"Who?" she asked, her brows in a V shape. She kept one hand on the pushcart and had dropped the other by her side.

"The lawyer. Dave the Rooster." I pointed and tried to remember the office number, since this building had a lot of offices leased by various other businesses.

"Him?" She rolled her eyes. "I told him that darn rooster had to go. I don't care if it does work for security at the airport. This is no place for a farm animal." She tsked and put her hand back on the pushcart to start walking again.

"I need the trash from his trash can." It was an odd thing to say, and by the way her eyes narrowed, she was trying to figure me out. "I'm Violet Rhinehammer with the *Junction Journal*."

I patted around my body to see if any sort of identification was on me, but I'd left my purse on Diffy's desk.

"Darren, can you go get my purse?" I asked when he rounded the corner. "It's on Diffy's desk."

He didn't say anything. He simply turned back to go get it.

"Anyway, that darn rooster." I stomped. "I've gotten so many anonymous tips from people in this very building about the rooster, and I thought I'd come by and take a look around."

"In the trash?" she asked. I could see she was almost buying what I was completely lying about.

"In the trash is where the best-kept secrets are, right?" I wiggled a brow and kept my eyes on her, even though she glanced past me and took in Darren.

He handed me my purse, and I opened it and took out my business card.

"See. I am who I said I was, and I'd really love to get a look in the trash. His trash. Diffy Delk's." I had gotten really good at realizing most people needed you to say exactly what you wanted specifically, not generally.

"Is it in here?" Darren had lifted his hands up to his chest like little dinosaur arms and pointed into the silver metal trash compartment on her cart like he didn't want to touch anything in there.

"Nope. I put his bag out in the dumpster already." She took a few steps forward, pushing the cart in front of her. "You're more than welcome to go outside and look through it. I can't stop you, and I didn't see you today."

"Thank you." I lingered and watched her slowly walk down the hall.

"You better hurry, though. It's dumpster day, and they show up right about now too." Her words made my eyes pop open and look at Darren.

We both ran down the hall and pushed out the doors of the building, dodging people as we hurried to the back.

"Did you hear that?" I felt a deep fright as if we were too late when I heard the eerie echo of a truck's beeping bouncing off the building walls.

"Hurry!" Darren pointed at the garbage truck down the alley of another building, which faced in our direction. The dumpster of Diffy's building was next.

"Me? Why do I have to go dumpster diving?" I snarled.

"Fine." He grabbed my hand and dragged me along with him. He took one side of the flimsy dumpster top, and I took the other. "One, two, three."

On the count of three, we lifted the lid and peered inside at all the bags.

We shrugged. I grabbed the lip of the top of the dumpster and hoisted myself up, flinging my leg over. I sank in the bags as the smell curled around my body.

The roar of the garbage truck was getting louder and louder. Each time it beeped, I knew it was emptying the dumpsters, which were all lined up one by one.

I'd been so busy tugging my shirt collar up over my nose that I hadn't realized Darren had gotten inside with me and was already ripping open the plastic garbage bags.

One after the other, we ripped through the first layer of bags.

"Here!" I yelled when I saw the half-eaten chocolate bunny through the thin plastic. I leaned over the dumpster's edge and was very happy to see the garbage truck was at least three other dumpsters away.

Darren had gotten out, and I tossed him the bag. He dropped it and put his arms in the air in an offer to catch me when I jumped out.

"Thank you." I looked into his deep eyes and saw a spark I didn't recognize before in them.

"You're welcome." His closed-mouth smile reached his eyes, then they shifted to a strand of my hair that touched my cheek. He reached up and plucked a piece of paper from it. "We shouldn't wear the trash," he teased and tossed the piece of paper back in the dumpster.

Beep, beep. The honk of the garbage truck horn and the driver yelling at us to move brought us out of the moment we seemed to be having.

"Let's go." Darren gripped the trash bag with one hand and my hand with his other hand.

Once we were around the corner of the building and away from the noise of the truck and the clanking of dumpsters being emptied, I said, "That was different."

"Violet Rhinehammer, every day is different with you." I wasn't sure if that was a compliment or not, but I definitely took it with some pride.

"At least I'm not boring." I laughed and led us down the sidewalk going toward Holiday Park.

You'd never have known a murder had taken place there earlier. The crime scene was still roped off with the streamers, and even though a judges' table was there this morning, it was all gone now, leaving the roped-off area nothing but a grassy patch where Frances Green's body had lain in the bunny suit.

"I still wonder why Frances was in a bunny suit." I shifted my focus from the tingling feeling of holding Darren's hand to why we were walking down the road toward Brewing Beans like we'd planned before our dumpster pit stop.

"I don't know, but I think we'll get some really good insider information from Owen tonight," he said and released some of the tension between our fingers before he completely dropped my hand.

"Hello, you two." Rhett Strickland, Darren's cousin, walked out of Flowerworks with a large bouquet in his hands. His eyes were still focused on Darren's hands and mine. "So you're really an item these days?"

"We are just..." I decided to help Darren out, even though it was at the risk of my own heart getting hurt. The two cousins had a history, and it wasn't any of my business. Though Darren seemed not to want anyone to see us holding hands, I thought protecting him was worth the cost.

"We were just going to get a coffee." Darren gripped the trash bag with both hands. "So we can stay up for our date tonight."

"Date. Huh." Rhett Strickland was a good-looking man. No doubt about it.

He had the perfect olive skin against his dark features. The dimples in his cheeks deepened when he smiled widely, but he wasn't smiling right now.

"Who's the lucky lady?" I was so taken aback by Darren's comeback about our date, I was a tad bit uneasy, since Rhett had tried to take me on a couple of dates when I first came to town.

Why couldn't he be the one to interest me? Nope. It had to be the mysterious cousin whose wounded heart stole mine.

"Fern. I thought I'd wish her luck on the welcome speech she has to give tomorrow to open the Hip Hop Hurray Festival." He and Fern Banks had been on and off for years. She was the local beauty queen and really did match him in the looks department.

"Tell her good luck from me, even though I'll be covering it for the newspaper." I offered a smile, but Rhett didn't return it. "Gotta go."

I took the first step between the cousins so I could get on with what mattered most to me right now.

Mama.

CHAPTER SIX

The Brewing Beans coffee shop was full of life for a late afternoon. I overheard whispers and low chatter about what'd happened to Frances as Darren and I made our way up to the counter, and I figured that was why everyone had gathered.

Nothing went better with gossip better than a hot cup of coffee.

A few copies of this week's *Junction Journal* were still sitting on the counter next to the pastries, muffins, and biscuits when we finally made it through the crowd.

The baristas were too busy making drinks, taking orders, and ringing up purchases to even notice us.

"Hey, you two." Hazelynn Hudson, the owner, came out of the back of the coffee shop with a large jute bag of coffee beans ready for grinding. Hershal, her husband, took a pocketknife out of the front pocket of his jeans and ripped a hole in the bag. He helped Hazelynn lift the heavy sack up so they could pour some beans into the large grinder.

"I tell you what," Hershal said over the smell of the fresh beans that married with the baked goods, making my stomach growl. "We thought we were doing great when we offered holiday special brews, but nothing brings in a crowd better than a murder."

"You heard it was murder?" I asked, since I'd not realized Matthew

Strickland had any sort of press conference. I should know, since I was the only one from the paper who would get the assignment to show up.

"Not officially." Hazelynn playfully smacked her husband on the arm. "That's how rumors get started." The bangles and bracelets decorated with dangling enameled Easter eggs, bunnies, baskets, and religious pieces jingled up and down her wrists.

"Ouch, woman!" He laughed and rubbed the sting her hand left behind. "Why would they clear out the park if it wasn't suspicious? We aren't stupid."

Hershal leaned across the counter and dragged a tiered tray filled with brownies. As they got closer to me, the smell of dark chocolate was one I instantly recognized, and the cute little pink candies on top in the shape of a bunny formed a perfect crunch for the tasty treat.

"I can see you want one." Hershal knew my weakness. "A free dark chocolate brownie for some information."

"You naughty man." I winked. I tried to stay firm and not say a word until Darren reached over me and took one.

"Yep. It was murder," Darren said through a mouthful of chocolate.

"Darren." I shook my head. "The only reason we know is because they've taken Mama down to the station for questioning. I'm here to get some coffee to take over to Kristine, since she sits on the village council."

"She isn't on the village council," Hazelynn corrected. "Mayor Paisley goes to the meetings."

"Right, and I know Frances was on the council." I scanned the brownies to see which one was the biggest before I took one.

"Frances Green?" Hazelynn asked. "Is that who's dead?" Her thick brows jumped up on her forehead, and her egg earrings swung around from her earlobes.

"I thought you said you heard about the murder," I said over the hissing of espresso machines, the clinking of spoons against ceramic mugs, and the murmur of conversation from the customers behind us.

"We did, but we didn't know who until now." Hershal was bent over the hot, sudsy water in the sink, washing the mugs by hand before putting them on the drying rack. "My goodness. I guess someone got tired of Maximus Stone being the bunny every year and wanted a change."

"Maximus Stone?" I asked. Hazelynn gave me a fresh cup of coffee and patted my hand as she whispered that it was on the house. I mouthed a thank-you to her and still put a few dollars, which probably would've paid for the coffee and brownie, in the tip jar.

It was a little way to show how much I appreciated her kindness, even though she didn't require it. Sometimes it was nice to be recognized for such gestures. Hazelynn and Hershal had always been very kind to me.

"Mr. Stone has been the Hip Hop Hurray bunny for as long as I have been around. He's got to be at least seventy." Darren opened the lid of the cup of coffee Hazelynn had given him and doctored it up with a couple of sugar packets and some creamer.

The light background music playing and the sound of milk being steamed made it hard for me to hear everything Darren was saying, but I knew we had to put Mr. Stone on our list.

"Let me get you some fresh creamer." Hazelynn took the creamer pitcher right out of Darren's hand and hurried down to the mini refrigerator located underneath the counter.

"Do you know Mr. Stone?" I asked Darren. He nodded and blew on the hot coffee before he took a sip.

He made a sour, awful-looking face.

"Definitely needs more cream." He shivered.

"Back to Maximus Stone." I leaned closer to him and said, "What if he wasn't going to be the bunny this year? What if those are his toes in the photo of Mama at the judges' table, and he saw the score sheet?"

"Who has those score sheets?" he asked, though he did not direct his question to me specifically.

"The only person we can ask that's not in jail is Emily." I blinked a few times, thinking Emily was much more important than going to see Kristine. "Hazelynn?" I got her attention just as she put down the creamer for Darren. She would run off to help one of the baristas soon. "What is Emily's absolute favorite item on your menu?" I asked.

Darren's phone rang, and he held up his finger to me while he exited the coffee shop to take it.

"This week, she's been gobbling up the Hip Hop Cake Pop." I smiled as she said the name.

"I'll take six to go." I pulled out more cash and put it on the counter. No way would I let her give those to us. When she started to protest, I said, "I won't hear of it. You have to make a living just like us."

Hazelynn quickly boxed up the cake pops. Darren was waiting for me outside.

"I'll pick you up tonight for our date." Darren smiled, making me feel better than the tasty chocolate brownie had. He said, "I've got to get back to the bar. There's a delivery I need to sign for. If Otis is there, I'll ask him a bunch of questions."

"I thought you mentioned something about going there after we eat." I wanted to be clear that I intended to ask Otis some questions too. Darren handed me the trash bag with the half-eaten bunny inside.

"You never know what the night might bring." Darren winked, letting me know he might have some other ideas up his sleeve.

"I want to find out who is framing Mama," I called out to him when he proceeded toward the park. "It looks like I'm on my own," I muttered and turned to walk a couple of shops down to Emily's Treasures.

"Good afternoon." When I got there, Emily waved from across the small boutique over the racks of clothes. "I've got some great Easter dresses." She pointed at the wall with the large display of Easter eggs and streamers above a line of dresses all neatly organized by soft pale colors.

"Actually…" I made my way around the racks of clothes, though I did stop and look at a cute hot-pink three-quarter-length sweater that would be great for my date tonight. I plucked the hanger off the round rack and draped the sweater over my arm. "I came to see you."

I plunked the box of Hip Hop Pop Cakes on the counter.

"And what do I owe this pleasure?" Emily eyeballed the sweater. "I've already marked it down as low as I can."

"This. Nope. I'm good with the price you have on it." I smiled and held it up to my face. "Do you think it's too much with my hair?"

"You have gorgeous blond hair even Fern Banks fawns over. If you cut a hole in this box and hung it over your shoulders, it'd look good." Emily was so sweet. "What's up?"

Emily removed one of the cake pops from the box and took a bite.

"Matthew Strickland took Mama in for questioning after he got statements from everyone there."

"What?" She put the uneaten remainder of the cake pop back in the box and tried to swallow what was in her mouth. "Has he lost his mind?"

"I don't know." I shook my head. "I just know that Mama had no real motive other than the baking competition to have wanted to murder Frances."

"This is ridiculous, though Frances did tell me not to take any of Millie Kay's chocolate Easter bunnies because they were awful." That didn't make me feel any better.

"Then why on earth would she be eating one when she—" I clicked my tongue in a gesture representing murder instead of saying the word in front of the customers milling around us.

"That wasn't Millie Kay's. Someone had left one at her spot on the judges' table." Emily's little bit of information just might be the clue I needed to show Mama didn't kill Frances. "We get little treats left behind every year."

"What did she do with Mama's?" I asked.

"I have no clue, but she grabbed the one left on her score sheet and went off to get on that goofy suit she likes to put on." Emily had all the answers to many of my questions.

"She put on a bunny suit every year?" I asked, remembering how I'd counted seven bunnies, again making Frances one. But we already knew that.

"Yes. She likes to start the final hop of the competition. At least that's what she called it." Emily took a couple of steps down the counter and rang up a customer while she told me about how things had been run years past. "Since she was the head judge, she wanted to have a lot of pageantry, wearing a costume and hopping in with the final five behind her. She wanted to show them how they needed to perform for the final in order to win."

There was a lot to unpack, and I was going to dissect it piece by piece.

Starting with the last statement, I asked, "You said she needed them to perform a certain way. What does that mean?"

"Thank you," she told the customer and handed them the cutest white bag with their purchase inside underneath a slew of orange tissue paper. "Happy Easter!"

She came back down and stood in front of me.

"Yes. She wanted them to not only look good but also be playful with the children, to act engaged and use their paws to exaggerate expressions, since you can't really see their faces." In no certain terms, she was telling me that Frances required things to be how she wanted them.

Control.

"You also mentioned five finalists. When I was taking photos for the paper, I counted seven." I watched the confusion linger on her face.

"No. No. There were five." She was adamant and started to count off by name. "Owen, Maximus Stone, Nathan Brown, Gabriel Knighton, and Thea Chase. Don't forget Frances was in one too."

"I got her, and she would make six. There are clearly seven bunnies in the photos." I wished I'd brought the photos with me, but I hadn't.

"We have all of their applications and photos of them in costumes." She hit the nail on the head for me. "I have Frances's bag with me."

"Matthew didn't take it?" I asked.

"No. He wanted me to clear out the judges' table so they could get it out of the way, and I just grabbed up everything that was mine and hers. Millie Kay had already gotten her baking box, and I saw her standing with you." She looked around before she called out to one of her clerks to watch the floor while she took me to the office.

"Here you go." She set the leather briefcase on the desk. "I don't know the combination, but you're more than welcome to take this to Matthew if you think it'll have some clues. I'm swamped here or I would do it."

"I'd love to take it to Matthew," I said, but I thought, *after I take a crack at trying to open it.* "Another thing you said struck me. You mentioned that there was a chocolate bunny on her judge's sheet."

"That's right." Emily nodded, and the office door opened. Her daughter Katie rushed inside. "Katie, say hello to Ms. Rhinehammer."

"You can call me Violet," I told her.

"How were your piano lessons?" Emily asked her daughter. They talked about a piece she'd been practicing in A minor before Emily told Katie, "Ms. Rhinehammer brought some Hip Hop Cake Pops on the counter."

Katie ran out of the office, leaving Emily and me to finish up the conversation.

"I'm sorry about that. She should've knocked." Again, Emily was sweet.

"Oh no. No apology needed. Family first. That's why I'm here. To help get Mama free of these charges." I took a breath to refocus on what I was asking before Katie came in. "You mentioned the chocolate bunny?"

"Yes. She unwrapped it and took a big bite of the bunny tail. We laughed, but she moaned about how good it was and then hurried off to get into the outfit, taking it with her." Emily's eyes grew. "She did say when she was walking away that if whoever made this bunny was in the Bake-Off, she might have some competition. And something about not tossing this one."

"Bake-Off. Tossing." The words made me think of the Incubator and when Mama gave her chocolate bunny to Frances. "Did Frances take a bite of Mama's bunny on the way to Holiday Park and toss it in one of the trash cans on her way?" I asked under my breath.

"What? I didn't hear you." Emily tilted her head with her ear slightly more toward me.

"Thank you. You've been a big help." I grabbed the briefcase and the trash bag. "I'll get this to Matthew."

I didn't tell her when I would get it to Matthew, but it was getting late.

I paid for my sweater, and when I walked out of Emily's Treasures, I saw I'd gotten a phone call from my dad, saying Mama had been released to home confinement until they decided whether to bring charges against her.

There was no way I would let that happen, even if I had to use a knife to break into Frances's briefcase to see if it held any clues.

CHAPTER SEVEN

The normal thing to do would be to go home, check on Mama, and tell her my game plan, even though I'd yet to have one I was comfortable telling her, since she had a big mouth and could cause more harm than good.

Telling Mama would be the normal thing, and so would going on a real date with Darren. No. I couldn't be normal. I couldn't even say that going back to the office and writing down everything I'd learned since I'd left the office earlier with Darren was for Mama.

It was, but to be perfectly clear, I had a problem. I couldn't deny myself the adrenaline rush I got from putting together clues to come up with other suspects and motives for Frances's murder.

I already had a sweater to wear. I did keep extra clothes at the office, something I'd learned to do years ago while working back home. At any given moment, I could spill something on what I was wearing. Similarly, at any given moment, a press conference could be called. I wasn't about to get caught unprepared for a press conference.

I wasn't sure what pants were at the *Junction Journal* office, but there had to be something that went with the hot-pink sweater so I didn't have to go back home.

When I opened the jiggle joint's door, the darkness of the bar pierced my eyes as the late-night sun skittered across the ocean and found a place to land.

I took the garbage bag, the shopping bag, and the briefcase into one hand while I fanned away a mix of alcohol, perfumes, colognes, and cigarette smoke with the other.

Too bad I couldn't plug my ears from the thunderously loud music and the roar of the excitement from the crowd as the dancer strutted across the stage.

"What are you doing here?" Darren hollered from the other side of the bar. He was filling up a stein with a beer on tap.

"I wanted to tell you that I'll meet you at your house instead of you picking me up." The lighthouse, Darren's home, was right here on the beach. It was a very cool tourist attraction, and people took a lot of group photos there.

"I want to write down all the clues we got." I held up the briefcase and tried really hard not to look at the woman on the stage, who was dressed as an Easter Bunny—but not like the Easter Bunnies we were investigating. "Emily told me the five finalists. And the list is in this briefcase. The winner is in here."

"So there were five plus Frances." Darren grabbed the rag from under the counter and swiped it along the bar top. He didn't seem to share my excitement about the contents of the leather box. "Do you want something to drink, and we can discuss here?"

"No. I want to write it all down and look over it."

My friend back home, Mae West, came to visit me, and while she was here, we'd gotten caught up into another crime.

Mae was very nosy and a busybody, so she went hog wild trotting all over Holiday Junction, looking for clues. The one thing I took away from her was that she'd write every little detail down. As a journalist, we liked the large story—the grand ideas and theories—but Mae said all the details were in the little things. She was right.

"It's too important to me now that Mama is on house arrest," I told Darren. He met me with a nod, which made it appear he'd not heard.

After I saw the wounded look in his eyes, I asked, "No word from your dad?"

"Nope." He tossed the wet rag back from where he'd gotten it. "I thought after he asked us to look into the last homicide, he'd come back to ask for some help this time."

"We don't need his permission. It's you and me." I lifted my hand up and over the bar top and placed my hand on his. "We still on for supper?"

"When are you going to learn to say 'dinner'?" He answered my question with a question. "We have breakfast, lunch, and dinner."

"I have breakfast, dinner, and then supper." I mocked him with a flirty smile that I knew sent him spiraling by that knowing look in his eyes and the way his lips curved up at the edges. With my elbows up on the edge of the bar, I curled up on my toes as if I was about to go in for a little kiss. He leaned in.

I turned my head to look down the bar before he could kiss me.

"I see Owen is down there," I said.

"You little minx, you." Darren smacked the top of the bar with his fingers. "Supper." He mimicked me. "Be at my house or else."

"Or else what?" I joked and saw Owen was having a beer. "Can I get a beer like Owen's?"

"You mean can you buy Owen a beer?" he said to correct me, since he knew I wasn't big on going to bars, or even drinking, for that matter.

"You know what I mean." I glared before I broke out into a big grin, wiggled my brows, and made my way down to where Owen and Shawn were sitting on their usual stools.

"I'm glad this Easter Bunny didn't get murdered." I put a hand on Owen's back.

"I can't believe someone didn't kill her already." Owen snorted. His lips pursed and his brows dipped when Darren slid the beer across the bar top to him. Darren pointed at me. "I guess you want this on the record?"

"No. I want you to tell me exactly what you had to do to get to the top five. I want you to tell me why you think someone wanted to murder Frances, since my mama seems to be Matthew's number-one suspect because of the poisoned chocolate bunny."

"Frances had a very strict list of rules." Owen picked up the beer mug and took a gulp.

"Like what?" I needed the complete details.

"We had to do this little hop."

"Plus the wave. Don't forget the wave." Shawn, who liked to refer to himself as the Tooth Fairy, nudged Owen.

"Yeah, that too." Owen snickered and haphazardly pointed at Shawn. "The first tryout, we all had to stand in a line with our outfits on and do the wave. If she didn't like the look of your paw, then she kicked you out. Luckily, I had good paws."

"The hop?" I questioned.

"Yeah. The wave was for the parade. The hop was when you took a break and had to hop away from the bunny chair. She didn't want the rabbit to walk away but hop. Like this." He drew his hands up to his chest. "Then, before we were supposed to disappear behind the curtain, the bunny was meant to stop and give a little shake of the tail."

"Curtain?" I asked.

"Yeah. They have a tent for when the bunny needs a break. Can you imagine sitting in that suit all day long, sweating and having those kids climb all over you?" He made it sound awful.

"Why would you want to try out for something that sounds so terrible?" I asked.

"I'm the Easter Bunny, remember?" He snorted and went back to his beer.

"Did you ever hear anyone give her a death threat or complaint? Any motive?" I was willing to take anything.

"No. But we five sure were excited to be asked back. And I think Nathan Brown had a shot at knocking Maximus Stone off the top spot. At least that was what we'd heard. They did the final judging a few nights ago, so today was the announcement. Though, technically, the final judging was supposed to be today." He caught my ear when he told me the final stage of judging was a few nights ago.

"So the bunnies knew they were there just to hear who the winner was?" I wondered how that could be, since Mama thought she was there to judge the final stage of competition.

"A little-known Frances secret." Owen shrugged.

"And Maximus Stone might've lost?" I asked and looked at Owen more closely. I couldn't tell drunk Owen from sober Owen, and from the way he knocked down the beers, I wasn't sure which one was talking to me and possibly getting things confused.

Honestly, I wasn't putting too much faith in what he was telling me. I wasn't going to ignore it entirely either. I'd let his words simmer in the back of my head.

"Told ya," Darren blurted out. "I told Violet at Brewing Beans that Maximus Stone was the bunny when we were kids."

"The other four of us didn't really care so much about the bunny but about the competition it was going to be to knock Maximus off the bunny trail." Owen shrugged. "I guess they won't have an Easter Bunny this year."

"Why not?" I asked, since I'd not heard that either.

"Everyone is afraid someone is trying to kill the bunny." Owen shook his head. "I've hung up my bunny ears."

I was about to leave, but Owen stopped me. "You mentioned chocolate bunnies and poison," he said. "She had a chocolate bunny in her hands and dropped it as soon as I smacked right into her when I left this place to go to the audition. I apologized, but she thanked me. Said it was the worst bunny she'd ever eaten."

"Did she leave it on the ground?" I asked.

"Nah. You know Frances. All tidy and whatnot. She picked it up and threw it in the trash can right outside the door." Owen had been more help than he knew.

"Thank you." I threw my arms around his neck. "Thank you!" I called again, sprinting to the door as fast as my legs could carry me. "I'll see you at your house, Darren!"

I hit the door, opening it. With what little light was left in the day before the sun sank down into the ocean, I ran over to the garbage can closest to the bar.

"There you are." A big sigh of relief came over me when I looked inside and saw the half-eaten bunny face with one candy eye staring up at me. "Now we have all but the one in Mama's baking box."

I found a tissue in the bottom of my purse and carefully reached down into the trash can to retrieve the bunny. There had to be some sort of saliva on it to prove it was the one Frances had bitten into and that the little candy eyes were the ones Mama used.

There were so many questions that needed answering and that I had to get out of my head. I walked along the sidewalk to the *Junction Journal* office with the briefcase, the trash bag, the three bunnies we'd gotten back from Goldie, and the half-eaten bunny in my grip.

I carefully put them all on the table in the office kitchen. I wasn't convinced I should look in the briefcase or tell Matthew I had it. I left the trash bag from Diffy's office, Goldie's bunnies, and the bunny I'd retrieved from the trash can outside the jiggle joint on the table. Then I took the briefcase into the office.

The whiteboard had all the bullet points Darren had written on it. After leaving the briefcase where it was, I walked over, picked up the dry-erase marker and made a list of more suspects than just Mama.

"Maximus Stone," I wrote down. Under his name, I wrote a possible motive. "He wasn't going to win. He had previous experience of Frances in a bunny suit, so he gave her the Easter bunny because he knew it was her favorite candy."

The more I talked it out, the more of a theory I formulated, and the surer I was that Maximus Stone killed Frances.

"First-degree murder," I wrote. I circled the phrase a few times because if he did it, his actions were premeditated. He poisoned the bunny, knowing she'd eat it.

I took a step back and thought about Nathan Brown. I had no motive for him, but I was sure to pay him a visit.

"Emily said Thea Chase, Owen, Maximus Stone, Nathan Brown, and

Gabriel Knighton were the five." I went back to my computer to bring up the photos. "Who is the sixth person? The killer?"

I went back to the whiteboard and looked at the photo Darren had taped up, showing Mama sitting at the judges' table. The photo with the bunny toe sticking ever so slightly inside it. When I took a closer look at the table, I saw a chocolate bunny between Mama and Emily.

It had to be the one that poisoned Frances.

"The briefcase." When I jerked back to look at it, my hair flung around my face. "Emily also said all the contents for the contestants were inside."

I laid the briefcase on its side, bent down at eye level, and looked at the lock. I reached out to touch the combination numbers, wanting to roll them into some sort of random number in hopes it was the key, but I pulled back.

"Oh." I flung my hands in front of me like I was throwing away the bad deed of breaking into something that wasn't mine.

I stood up and paced back and forth.

"What if the answer to whose toes those are is in there?" I chewed on the inside of my cheek. The stress fell over me, and I sucked in a deep breath and blew it out slowly, like I'd heard so many people in the health industry tell me in interviews on how to manage stress.

"That's not working." I stopped and glanced back over at my desk. I was torn between the little angel on my shoulder telling me to be a good girl and the devil sitting on the other side saying I'd always been a good girl, and where did that get me?

Holiday Junction.

"It's for Mama." I pulled the letter opener out of my pen holder sitting on the desk and went at the briefcase like I was about to have a sword fight with it. "I'll win," I told the leather box before I stuck the tip of the letter opener in the keyhole, popping the darn thing open.

One by one, I took out the file folders, making a stack. The only thing I didn't see was the final winner sheet Emily said she thought would've been in there.

"Gabriel Knighton." I was saying the names written on the front of each folder. "Maximus Stone, Nathan Brown, Thea Chase, Owen."

Since these people were my only suspects, I left the remaining files in the briefcase for now and decided to continue what Darren had done —post a photo by each name.

"You're first, Maximus." I opened his file and carried it over to the white board. Just like Emily said, there were a couple of photos—one of him wearing the entire bunny outfit and one with the head stuck up underneath his arm. "Where's the feet?"

I thumbed through the folder when I saw the photo stopped at the bunny's knees. I reached back to get the other four files, and when I looked through them, the photos showed the contestants in the same poses.

"How am I going to see if the toes match?" I wondered and knew there was only one thing I could do. "I'll have to pretend to interview them like I'm doing some sort of story for the *Junction Journal*."

Somehow, I would have to get in front of each one of them and try to see their suit. The idea felt really risky, like I was bait for the killer. But I knew what had to be done.

After all, it was for Mama.

CHAPTER EIGHT

"The top five weren't the only files in there!" I yelled into the crack of Darren's bathroom door. I had to holler over the shower noise for him to hear me. "There were more, and you won't believe who one of them is."

I put my ear up against the door of the bathroom. All I could hear was water hitting the shower door.

"Here are the names—Julian Storm, Mason Backwood, and Curtis Robinson." I took a particular interest in the last one. "Curtis Robinson!" I repeated more loudly to make sure he heard me.

When I said the coroner's name that second time, a twinge of something stung my intuition.

"You know, I did notice at the scene he was visibly more upset than the other murder victims I'd seen him standing over," I mumbled, backing away from the door when I heard the bathroom doorknob twist to open.

"What did you say?" Darren walked out with a towel around his waist and his chest bare for my eyes to see. He raked another towel over his hair then wiped out his ears.

"I said that, um…" My mouth dried, as did all my brain cells.

Momentarily.

"I said Curtis Robinson had tried out for the bunny, and he sure didn't mention anything like that at the scene." I blinked a few times and busied myself with the files.

Who was I kidding? I looked out of the corner of my eye to sneak another look at Darren's six-pack abs before he walked into his room and left the door open a crack.

I leaned a little to the right to get a look inside before I jerked back.

"What's wrong with you, Violet Rhinehammer?" I muttered in frustration, my cheeks puffing out as the air in my lungs flowed out of my mouth in one long steady stream.

"Maybe because he didn't see any reason to say anything. I mean, did Julian Storm come forward with any information, or whoever else's name you rattled off?" He walked out with a pair of jeans, wet hair, and a black long-sleeved shirt he was currently buttoning up.

His fingers didn't work quickly enough, giving me one last little peek of those abs.

"Right?" He walked barefooted across the round interior of the lighthouse he'd remodeled into a home.

Darren sat down on the custom-made semicircular sofa underneath the windows. Over his shoulder, I could see out over the sea. The view was gorgeous during the day, but at night, it was downright spectacular.

You'd think it would be dark. It wasn't. The ocean was vast, expansive, and dotted with the distant lights of boats or ships. Even though it was a little shaky here on land, given what was going on in the village with Frances's murder, the surface of the water was smooth and still and reflected the moonlight and stars.

The lighthouse beam would shine out across the water, illuminating a circular path and creating a moving pattern of light and shadow on the ocean's surface.

"Earth to Violet." Darren had already put on his shoes and ran his hand through his hair, giving it his messy touch while I'd gotten lost in the view. "Did you hear what I said?"

"I'm sorry. I didn't." I turned back and smiled at him. "I feel so alive when I see the stars. When I lived back in Kentucky, you know I lived in the middle of a national forest where the stars were the lights at night. It was so breathtaking. I remember thinking the night before I left to get on the airplane to that job interview in California that I was going to miss the stars. From what I know, a big city and its lights make it hard for stars to be seen properly."

I turned back to look out once more before it was time for us to go on our date.

"Here you are." He came up from behind me, wrapped both arms around my waist, and rested his chin on my shoulder. Our eyes caught in the reflection of us standing there, holding on to each other. "I'm glad you're here."

His heart hammered against my spine.

I turned my body around, his hands staying clasped around my waist, and looked up at him. My cheeks flushed pink.

He must've noticed. He grinned and placed one of his hands on my neck, and his thumb caressed my cheek.

My skin prickled from his touch.

Or maybe it was Darren's leaning down that made my body inwardly shudder.

My phone rang, jerking us apart before our lips touched.

"I don't think we are meant to kiss." He lifted his arm and ran his hand through his hair in frustration.

"Mama?" I answered. "What's wrong?"

She told me Chief Strickland had just called a press conference.

"At this hour?" I asked, wondering why I, the editor of the *Junction Journal*, had not gotten the usual text message with all the updates. "In front of the Holiday Park?"

Mama confirmed that.

"Let me guess. No dinner either?" Darren asked, his jaw hardened.

"No supper either. Let's go." I grabbed the briefcase and headed to the door, his heavy footsteps behind me.

"A nighttime press conference is unusual, right?" I asked Darren.

It was a strange spring night, thanks to the warmer weather. Even the breeze coming off the ocean and circling around my ankles on the path leading up to Holiday Park was warm.

"Yeah. I wonder why he didn't wait until tomorrow," Darren pointed out. "I was really looking forward to spending time with you."

"Me too," I said and picked up the pace. "I wonder if Curtis will be there. I really want to ask him about the competition and what he thought about Frances."

"I really love a good garlic sauce, and I heard Carnevale had a really good one." Darren shuffled alongside me.

"There's really no clear motive, but we have to get a look at the bunny feet. And the chocolate bunny Frances was eating." It dawned on me that Mama didn't say a word about the warrant the police had to search her house and how that went. "I wonder if they found anything in the chocolate she had at home. I'm telling you, we need to get these bunnies to your dad so he can test them. I wished I'd brought them with me."

"Even the atmosphere is supposed to be pretty romantic," Darren murmured.

"What?" I stopped in front of the fountain and couldn't prevent myself from looking over to the grassy area where Frances had died. It was too dark to see over there, but I knew the general direction.

"Carnevale," Darren said with a little more passion. "I was really looking forward to taking you out on a real date."

"I'm sorry you're disappointed, Darren Strickland, but there's one thing you need to know," I huffed as I picked up my pace even more. "When you date a southern girl, you date her family. Right now, the only person we need to be concerned about is Mama."

"Date? Are we dating?" he asked.

Luckily, it was dark, and the stretch of the park we were walking through to get to the police department was pitch black, other than the stars overhead. However, if looks could kill, as the phrase goes, Frances

TONYA KAPPES

Green wouldn't've been the only resident dead before the clock struck midnight.

I didn't even give him the satisfaction of or waste my breath on responding to him.

"I oughta kick my own self," I muttered, leaving him trailing behind me. My arms pumped like I was one of those speed walkers. "For even thinking you and I could be a couple."

"Violet, you're too sensitive." Every word that came out of his mouth felt like a dart.

I stopped, my back to him. He tumbled around me and looked at me.

"See." I gestured between us. "This is why we weren't meant to kiss. The stars know we aren't aligned. Thank you, stars!" I called out and took the necessary steps to move around him.

"Come on, Violet." He squirmed. "Don't tell me you believe in all that junk about things written in the stars. All of that is mumbo jumbo."

"Whatever." I put my hand up but increased my pace to a slight jog when I saw Matthew had already taken to the podium they'd put out for the press conference.

A few of the surrounding villages and their reporters were already set up and facing him.

"We have some good evidence collected at the scene of Ms. Green's death. We have one person of interest and truly believe this is an isolated incident," Matthew said to the press.

I barely made it in time to pull my phone out and tap the voice memo to record him so I could get all the facts he was willing to give to the public and write an article on them when I went back to the office in the morning.

"Can you give us the name of the person of interest?" one of the reporters shouted out.

"We can't do that at this time, since it's still considered an active investigation because we are still collecting evidence." He scanned the crowd for more questions.

"I understand you issued a search warrant," I yelled out.

"Who said that?" Matthew looked around.

"Violet Rhinehammer, *Junction Journal*!" I threw my arm up in the air and waved the phone around. "We can say that I went to get the public record of the search warrant, but truth be told, it was to my mother, Millie Kay Rhinehammer's, home."

A hushed chatter grew over the reporters as they had their cameramen move. All of them started to surround me.

"Can you confirm if you found anything in Millie Kay Rhinehammer's home? That's Millie, M-I-L-L-I-E," I said, spelling it out for the reporters to write down her name correctly. "Sometimes people spell it with a Y, but it's I-E." I smiled for the cameras. "There's no evidence other than that the victim died clutching a chocolate bunny. Millie Kay Rhinehammer did make a batch of chocolate bunnies, but it's also a fact that chocolate bunnies are made and sold this time of the year." I snickered and shrugged before I continued speaking.

"It is Easter. Who doesn't have chocolate bunnies around? Especially during the Hip Hop Hurray Festival. Or is it just Millie Kay?" I asked with a lot of sarcasm in my tone.

"Answer Violet's question." Darren stood tall next to me and held my hand, even though we'd just had what I'd call a fight. "The public deserves to know if the person of interest, in this case Millie Kay Rhinehammer, had evidence in her home."

The reporters shoved their microphones back in front of Matthew.

"We aren't going to elaborate on the details of what we found in Mrs. Rhinehammer's home, but we can say we did find some evidence related to the victim."

All the reporters swung their microphones back at Darren and me.

"Have you arrested Mrs. Rhinehammer?" Darren asked.

"No." Matthew's one-word reply told the group gathered in front of him in no uncertain terms that they didn't have enough to bring a murder charge against her.

"Then it seems to me there are more persons of interest to find." I talked into my phone and then held it up for any more comments from the chief. "Do you have anything to say to the residents and tourists in Holiday Junction?" I asked.

"This is being considered an isolated incident," he stated again. "The Hip Hop Hurray Festival will take place as planned. The Bake-Off, the Easter Bunny, and the final festival party where the village Merry Maker posted the sign will also go on as planned."

"Who is playing the Easter Bunny?" I asked, wondering if he was going to name the winner, since there was no winner's list in the briefcase like Emily had thought.

"The entire Village Council will be hosting an open audition tomorrow at Holiday Park." Matthew and I gave each other one last long stare before I started to walk off, Darren behind me. "If all of you want to report on that, we'd love for there to be hundreds of people trying out as this year's Hip Hop Hurray Festival bunny."

"Is there going to be more of a police presence?" I heard one of the reporters ask, but I didn't hear his answer because I was so wrapped up in my swirling thoughts.

"I have to go to the bunny auditions," I said and made a left to walk back home, since I was so close.

"Where are you going?" Darren asked.

"I'm going home. I need to make a plan and get a costume." My eyes darted about as I wondered how I was going to score an Easter Bunny costume. "Do you think Owen will let me borrow his suit?" I asked Darren in all seriousness.

"That's the funniest thing I think I've ever heard." Darren cackled like I was a loon. "You in a bunny outfit?"

"What? You don't think I could pull it off?" I questioned him. "I just want to hop around and be nosy. Try to hear things."

"You don't like to sweat." Darren had gotten to know me all too well.

"You're right, but I'll do just about anything for Mama." I bit my lip to keep from saying something I would regret later. Then Darren did the Darren thing he always did.

"I'll do anything for you and Millie Kay." He stopped laughing and put his hand on my arm, which he gave a light squeeze. "I'll dress up and do the audition. I'm sorry about earlier. I just want to spend some time alone with you. If that means taking on another murder investigation, call me Sherlock."

"Okay, Sherlock." I looked up at him. "I'll see you tomorrow."

I wiggled my nose.

"You do a cute bunny impression." He winked and gave me a slight wave goodbye as I walked opposite Darren and toward my house on Heart Street.

CHAPTER NINE

On normal nights when I walked home, I made a list of things I was grateful for while I took in the peaks and ridges of the mountains in the distance.

Not tonight.

I was anxious and wanted to hurry back home so I could form a solid plan. I was a planner, and it made me feel like I was getting somewhere with the case if I had a list of people to see.

The noise of loose stones or something crunchy or stepped on made me bolt around. The streetlights and porch lights were on at some of the houses, casting a soft glow over the empty sidewalk.

I turned back around and looked off into the distance at the outlines of the peaks and ridges against the dark sky, with the twinkling stars and now the crescent moon.

I got lost looking at the moon, thinking of how it was funny that it had started over the ocean when I was at Darren's house but now seemed to be giving off enough light for me to get home.

Feeling a little less anxious and more confident that I didn't hear footsteps, I proceeded down the sidewalk, where I could see the small sign for Heart Street.

My ears perked up when I heard the same noise again. The background noises of the crickets chirping, leaves rustling in the soft breeze, and the distant hum of a couple of cars weren't enough to mask the sound of footsteps.

"Who's there?" I jerked around, turning my head left and right. An uneasy feeling started in the base of my heart and trickled slowly into my gut. "I know you're there!"

Whoever it was needed to know I heard them.

"I have my phone, and I'm going to call Matthew Strickland. The chief of police!" I hollered and held my phone in my hand. The sound of footsteps got closer and closer until someone finally came into sight. "What do you want?" I yelled again.

"Huh?" the woman's voice asked. "Is that you, Violet?" I recognized the voice, but I wasn't sure from where.

"Who's there?" I called at the silhouette.

"It's me, Willow Johnson," she said. "Are you okay?" The heels of her shoes clicked against the pavement, gaining speed. She wasn't alone. She had a dog on a leash.

"I'm fine," I assured her. Finally, the outline of her face came into the shining lights of the streetlamps. "You scared me. That's all."

"I'm sorry." Her brows furrowed. "I was taking Pete for a walk. He has to go out before he can go to sleep or he will get me up a million times."

Pete sniffed my feet.

"Is he friendly?" I asked, something I did before petting any dog that wasn't familiar with me.

"Oh yeah. Super friendly." She held the leash taut. "Sit, Pete."

The sweet little scruffy brown-and-white pup sat down and put a paw up in the air.

"No shake. Just sit." Willow gave him one-word instructions. "We are learning tricks. I have him in a dog class. I just got him a few weeks ago from the animal shelter."

"You're a cute one, Pete." When I bent down, he took the liberty to jump to all four feet and give me one long lick across my face.

"Pete! No!" Willow gasped in horror, jerking his leash.

"Oh no. It's okay. I like dogs. I just don't have any." *Though it would've been nice to have one when I was thinking you were following me*, I thought but didn't say out loud because it would tell Willow I was being paranoid.

"I didn't, either, until a couple of months ago. There'd been a few more murders in the village, so I decided I should get a dog." She snickered and looked down at Pete. He'd lain down and had rolled over on his back with all four legs sticking straight up into the air. "He's not much of a watchdog."

"He's got personality. I like that." I laughed.

"What are you doing out here?" she asked. "Especially alone."

"I went to the press conference." I looked over my shoulder when I heard another noise and let go of the breath I was holding when I saw it was a cat darting off around a house.

Pete jumped to his feet, his floppy ears standing to life, but he didn't bark or attempt to chase the cat.

"Good boy, Pete," Willow told him in a baby voice and gave him a good scratch on the head. "I'm trying to teach him that we love all animals."

"It looks like it's working." I also gave him a pat. "Anyway, I've got to get going. I've got to work on a press conference article for the *Journal*."

"I'm sorry to hear about Millie Kay. I don't think she did it." Willow caught me off guard. "I heard she was taken into custody. You know how rumors get started around here."

"Yeah. I do." I shook my head. "I know Mama didn't do it, and I've got to figure out who did. I also don't think Chief Strickland has much against her or she'd be in jail."

"They let her go?" Willow asked. "That's good. I didn't hear that."

"It only happened a little bit ago. She's not off the hook. She's on house 'arrest.'" I put air quotes around "arrest," meaning it very loosely. "Really, they don't want her to leave town. Trust me, she's not leaving town. She didn't do it. I mean, there's a whole bunch of people who had some sort of disagreement with Frances. But the good news is the baking competition is still happening. Do you have something?"

"Yes." She didn't seem as enthusiastic as she did at the Incubator. "I keep thinking about Frances, though. She had the stove next to mine at the Incubator, and she was really helpful to me."

"I'm sorry. I didn't know you two had gotten close," I said.

She frowned and looked down. I could see her take a deep swallow like she was choking back tears that'd pooled in her throat.

"I didn't expect to be so upset over it, but she was really nice to me. I've dealt with her over the years for the Hip Hop Hurray Festival, and she never said an unkind thing to me." Willow looked up and blinked her big brown eyes a few times before she snorted. "Now, others weren't so lucky."

"Oh yeah?" I asked and decided I needed to hear exactly what kind of person Frances Green was. "Say, I'm heading home. I live in a remodeled apartment on Heart Street in the backyard of my parents' house. Do you and Pete want to come over for a little bit? I'll be more than happy to drive you home in Mama's golf cart."

"I don't know." She lifted the sleeve of her shirt. Her digital watch glowed the time. "It's only nine thirty. The darkness makes it seem so much later."

"Soon it'll be light at this time." Daylight saving time would soon be here, and it made nighttime in Holiday Junction so much fun. The days seemed longer because of the length of the sunlight. "You want to come?"

"I guess we could for half an hour or so." She gestured with her shoulders. "Does your mom care if Pete comes in?"

"He doesn't have to. She's got a really cool backyard with a firepit that'll be nice to sit around." I led the way down the sidewalk. "How is it that you know Frances Green so well? Something about the Hip Hop Hurray Festival?"

"Every year, Mr. Stone has been the Easter Bunny, and naturally, I help." She clicked her tongue for Pete to come on after he'd lingered a little too long sniffing the post of a mailbox.

"Maximus Stone?" I asked to make sure we were talking about the same person.

"Yeah." She nodded, and we turned right on Heart Street. "He's a great man."

"I guess I'm not following how you know him too." I pointed at the second driveway. "This is it."

"My goodness. I know it's dark, but I can see Millie Kay has put a lot of work into this house. I mean, look at that red door!" Willow ran to the front door, dragging Pete behind her. "I love red so much."

"Decades, maybe even centuries ago, southerners painted their door red if they had a paid-off house." I'd not even thought of that in a long time. "Not that Mama's trying to tell people here she's got a paid-off house. It's just one of her southern things."

"I work for him." Willow waited by the door.

"Work for who?" I asked and gave Mama's red door a hard knock.

"Maximus Stone." Willow answered the question I'd asked before she went all crazy over the red door. "I'm the secretary who keeps all of his appointments."

"Seriously?" I couldn't believe the gold I just hit. "Can you get me an interview with him?"

"Why?" she asked and turned toward the door as Mama swung it open.

"Hi there, Willow." Mama popped the door open like today was just a regular day in the life of a southern woman. "Come on in. Let me get the coffee cake out of the freezer."

"It's way too late for me to eat." Willow stepped inside before me. "Plus Pete and I were taking our nightly pee-pee walk before bedtime."

"Then you definitely need to refill those calories." Mama wasn't going to hear of it.

"Millie Kay." Willow held the leash close to her leg so Pete couldn't go very far from her. "This house. It's dramatically different. Gorgeous.'"

"Thank you, honey. I knew I had to have it the first time I laid my eyes on it. I said, 'Millie Kay, this is your new home.' Now…" Mama told her story while she got the Entenmann's crumb coffee cake out of the freezer.

Every southern woman kept an Entenmann's-brand dessert in her freezer or pantry at all times, just in case someone dropped in.

Mama lived for those times. And what little bit of joy Willow brought Mama by stopping in was actually very endearing to see.

"Mama, I thought we could sit by the firepit. Willow is Maximus Stone's secretary." I thought that was enough to stir some excitement into Mama, since we needed to interview everyone on the list of the top five bunnies.

Willow Johnson opened the door for me to get in front of Maximus Stone.

"That's nice, dear." Mama cut a couple of slices of the cake and put them in the microwave to thaw. "Decaf or regular?" Mama pointed at the coffee single-serve.

"Decaf?" Willow questioned and looked at me with a grin.

"You won't be leaving in half an hour," I told her, gesturing to the way things were already going with the coffee cake and now the coffee.

"Regular with a little cream." Willow patted Pete. "Do you have a bowl I can put some water in for Pete?"

"We will get one outside." I waved for Willow and Pete to follow me out the double sliding doors Mama had Daddy install once he moved to Holiday Junction.

"Is this new?" Willow asked about the sliders. "I love it."

"If you think that's something, wait until you see Violet's garage," Mama called over the hum of the single-serve coffee maker.

"Apartment, not garage," I corrected Mama once we got outside and lit the firepit with the easy-peasy push-button ignitor.

Mama's outdoor living area was truly a paradise and an extension of her home. She changed the cushions and decorations to go along with the holidays and seasons here in Holiday Junction.

"Pete can get up on the couch," I told Willow when I saw her try to keep him off the comfortable couches that weren't just comfy but stylish.

The cushions were in shades of yellow, turquoise, and coral, adding pops of color to the space. The air was filled with the sweet scent of jasmine and lavender Mama had planted in her small garden, making the atmosphere deeply relaxing. In the center of the area, a firepit crackled, creating a warm glow that lit up the space as Willow and I sat there in silence until Mama came outside with a tray bearing more than just the coffee cake.

"Don't worry," Mama teased. "I left the poison out of this batch." She pointed at the chocolate Easter bunnies.

"Mama!" I gasped. "That's in bad taste."

"If I can't laugh at my own expense, then I'll sit in there and cry." Mama picked up one of the bunnies and bit off an ear. She stuck it toward Willow. "See, I wouldn't eat it if it were going to kill me."

"No thank you." Willow waved it away, and honestly, I wasn't sure, but I didn't think Willow thought twice about eating something from Mama's kitchen until Mama made a big deal about it. "My eyes are feasting on your colorful spring landscape. It's truly breathtaking."

Mama took her flowers seriously.

The flowers in bloom included red roses, pink peonies, and yellow daffodils. They were arranged in a beautifully manicured garden with a picturesque fountain and some Easter decorations she'd added for a festive touch. A large wreath made of brightly colored eggs hung on my apartment door, as did a plush Easter bunny that I hadn't put there.

On the outdoor family-style table, Mama placed a vase full of colorful tulips, painted eggs, and an Easter basket to complete the spring-inspired look.

"We were talking about Frances Green." I started the conversation because I wasn't in the business of making chitchat at ten o'clock at night.

"Oh, poor thing." Mama frowned and said, "I didn't kill her."

"I know that, Mama, but Willow is Maximus Stone's secretary. Willow, do you think I could get in to interview him for the paper and maybe ask him some questions?" I asked.

"It's not him you need to talk to." Willow forked a piece of the coffee cake then placed the plate on the coffee table. From the way she was eating, I could immediately see that she was a secretary. She took only one bite at a time and set her fork down between bites. She also crossed her legs at the ankles and gave her full attention.

Those were great qualities I'd always noticed when I was interviewing secretaries for articles. They were tidy and alert and paid attention to detail, especially the details of the boss's schedule. If I could get in front of Maximus, I knew he'd have some inside scoop about Frances after all these years.

Possibly someone from her past had killed her and had been lurking all this time to wait for the perfect opportunity. You just never knew.

"I did hear her on the phone with Thea Chase." Willow's jaw dropped. "Oh no." Her face paled. "I don't like to gossip."

"Bless her heart," Mama said in a sincere way and eased up on the cushion on the rattan couch. She leaned over to grab Willow's hand. "It looks like you just saw a ghost. Besides, honey, we don't call it gossiping. We call it praying."

She put a spin on gossip just to make Willow feel better. Mama was no different from any other southern woman out there. We all did it, but it was a great way to get clues, and I was here for it.

"I didn't see a ghost. I think I heard one. I think." Willow looked between Mama and me.

"A ghost?" I wondered if my assessment of Willow was less than entirely correct. Maybe she was slightly off her rocker.

"Not a ghost, then, but what is it called when something happens, and I should've made sure Frances was okay?"

"Foreshadowing?" I asked, not sure if that was what she meant.

"Why don't you just tell us what happened?" Mama appeared to be all cool, calm, and collected, but I knew she was fretting deep down.

"Frances was baking at the Incubator when Thea called her." Willow started to tell the story, but in Mama's fashion, she interrupted Willow.

"Thea Chase, the bunny contestant?" Mama asked and gently lifted the coffee cup to her lips, her pinky finger sticking way out.

"Yes," Willow confirmed.

Mama mumbled and grunted.

"Mama, please," I cried out to her. "Please let Willow finish her story."

A huge sigh escaped Mama, who put her cup down on the coffee table before she adjusted herself on the small outdoor sofa across from Willow. Now Mama appeared as though she was ready to be quiet and give her full attention.

"Frances asked me to hit the speaker button because her hands had batter all over them. So I did." The way Willow told the story made my stomach lurch. "She told Frances that she was going to make a motion for Frances to be removed from the Village Council because Frances had her hand in too many of the contests, and being a contestant was a conflict of interest."

Willow fluttered her hands.

"It was an icky conversation, and I was actually embarrassed for Frances. But Frances assured me that nothing would come of it, so I just forgot all about it until…" Willow paused. Then her response was crisp and to the point, almost on edge. "I went to the Green Eggs and Honey Bunny Rabbitry, and Frances was there. She was giving Thea the business and telling her that she would see to it that Thea never won a competition and would pay if she tried to get Frances off the council."

"The Green Eggs and Honey Bunny Rabbitry?" I asked to make sure I got the name right. It sounded like I needed to go there—as a journalist, of course—and see if anyone there had heard about this public argument.

"The bunny hatchery. The bunnies Maximus had in his basket for tryouts come from there. Then he gives them away to families." Willow just confirmed there were many possible suspects other than Mama.

"Are you willing to state that on record?" I asked.

"I, um, I." She squirmed uncomfortably.

"You can remain anonymous." I gave her the option, since I could see she was waffling.

"Sure. I don't see why not." She eased up on the edge of the couch and reached down and ran her hand over Pete's head. "Do you think I should tell Chief Strickland?"

"No." I shook my head and picked up the coffeepot Mama had brought out. "I see him all the time, so I'll be more than happy to relay the information to him."

There was no way I was going to tell him until I found out exactly what I needed to know to get the information that would prove Mama's innocence to him.

CHAPTER TEN

"Violet, we have to get a bunny," Mama insisted once Willow and Pete left.

"I'll go in the morning to talk to the owners to see if they overheard Thea and Frances. This is no guarantee."

I didn't want to get Mama's hopes up. That was never a good thing. Trust me, when I went out on my first and only date with the captain of the football team in college, Mama had already decided on what NFL team he was going to play for and where we were going to live. She also checked out the local school for her unborn grandchildren. I'd learned my lesson.

"You are staying right here in this house. Now go get in bed with Dad. I'm going to go on home." I hugged her just as my phone chirped with a text from the bag hanging off my shoulder.

"You can tell Darren I know he sneaks around here." She shook her head and walked around the back patio, where she turned off the lights as well as the firepit. "I know there's not a holiday every single week, even though you two act as if you're planning co-Merry Maker things."

"Shhh. You can't say that too loud." I put my finger up to my mouth and looked around. We might be in the safety of her backyard, but I knew ears were everywhere.

I wouldn't be the one to let the big secret about the Merry Maker slip. No way.

"It's Louise and Marge." I hit the text thread between my bosses and me. "They said there's nothing in the queue to go live for the online version of the *Junction Journal*." I typed out a text to reply and said to Mama, "I know I have something scheduled."

It was exactly what I'd told them, too, but I also told them I'd check. However, I didn't bring my laptop home like I usually did. That meant I needed to run to the office.

"What are you doing?" Mama asked when she saw me heading toward the gate.

"I've got to go back to work. Do you think I could borrow your golf cart?" I asked her.

"Of course you can. Let me get my purse." She held her finger up for me to wait.

"You can't go," I told her. "You're under house arrest."

"Piddle." She scoffed. "It's almost midnight. They have no clue. It's not like I'm wearing one of those monitoring thingies on my ankle. It's Holiday Junction, not Alcatraz."

She disappeared through the sliding back door only to quickly return with the small set of golf cart keys dangling from her fingers.

"No, Mama. You can't go." I went to take the keys, and she jerked them away, holding them in her fisted hand.

"If I don't go, neither does my golf cart." She gave a quiet snort in the back of her throat.

"Fine. I guess I'll be safe, since I'm staring at the killer on the loose." I started to open the gate lock.

"I'll stay in the golf cart," Mama called out in the dark. "It's just fresh air. I won't leave. Scout's honor."

With my hand on the gate, I turned back around and said, "Since when were you a scout?"

"Shush up and come on." She took her first step of freedom out of the gate and trotted ahead of me. "I'm still your mama."

"You can't keep using that on me. I'm almost thirty," I told her, watching her punch the garage-door code into the keypad. She kept a golf cart instead of a car in the garage.

"I'll be your mama forever." She gave me a hard point. "Don't you forget that."

And that was the end of that. At least for Mama it was, and I was counting on her to sit in the golf cart like she scout-honored me. If that was a thing. Soon I'd find that out.

"I was a little busy trying to get you out of jail and kinda left work." Not that I really had to explain to Mama why I'd left without my laptop and why we were driving in the dark to get it.

It wasn't like it was a long drive. We could use the path from Holiday Park down to the beach and get out at the lighthouse.

"Looks like your midnight caller is up." Mama pointed out that the lights inside Darren's house were on.

"He owns a bar that's probably not even closed yet." I gripped the wheel and told myself I wasn't going to discuss my love life or its potential with her. "Speaking of bars…" I glanced at her and smiled when the moon outlined her face, reminding me of my reflection in the mirror.

"No thank you. I can't go in." Mama held on to the golf cart handle.

"I'm not saying we are going to the bar. I was going to ask you about Owen, the Easter Bunny." I snickered when I said it because that was how he really did introduce himself to everyone, even Mama when she first showed up in Holiday Junction. "I need to borrow his bunny suit."

"Why?" Mama shifted, turning a little toward me. She held on with both hands when I shot the juice to the pedal to get us up to the cottage, which was a little hilly.

"Part of my day is going to be finding more suspects than you. That means dressing up as a bunny to audition. If no one knows it's me under there, they might be willing to discuss the murder." Darren had offered to dress up, but I wanted to do it and get the information firsthand.

I put the golf cart in park once we pulled up to the cottage, and I told Mama to stay put.

"I'll be back in a minute. We can talk about Owen then." I stood outside the golf cart, and against my better judgment, which said to bring her with me, I let her stay.

What kind of trouble could she get in at almost midnight in a golf cart?

I took my office key out of my bag and unlocked the door. It was too dark inside to see the light switch, so I ran my hand up the wall and flipped the switch when I felt it.

I looked back over my shoulder at Mama. She gave me a little wave.

"I'm still here!" she yelled sarcastically.

"She's going to be the death of me," I muttered to myself and walked into my office. "What in the world?"

I stalked over to the window to make sure I'd put it down. Many times I'd opened the window not only for the nice breeze that rolled off the ocean but the smell of the salt that seemed to feed my creativity.

The window was shut tight, so it didn't make sense that the files on my desk were thrown about.

The faint shuffling noise that followed was still loud enough to tell me I wasn't alone.

"Who's there?" I called. "Mama! I told you to stay put," I said with exhaustion and headed back to the kitchen just in time to see a shadow darting out the cottage's back door.

And it wasn't Mama.

The glass of the broken door pane glistened all over the kitchen's tile floor.

"Stop!" I yelled, running out the door after them like I'd be able to stop them if they had some sort of weapon. "Stop!"

I did have my shoulder bag, which I could use to knock them in the head, but it was a last resort.

The whiz of the golf cart starting off and zooming away broke the noises of the waves crashing against the beach.

"No." I gasped and ran around the cottage. The golf cart's taillights were vanishing down the hill, and the headlights of the vehicle bore down on the running silhouette in front. "Please don't run them over," I groaned and bent over at the waist, trying to catch my breath.

Heaving, I stood back up and put my hands on my hips as I sucked in the fresh air. Then I noticed the golf cart roll as soon as Mama ran over the curb to continue the chase.

"Mama!" I screamed, forgetting I was already out of breath. I darted off toward her, the golf cart's undercarriage staring me in the face. "Mama!"

"Good grief. I'm night blind." Mama was pinned underneath the cart. A little blood trickled from her head. "I'm fine. Just pull this thing off me."

"I'm going to have to call an ambulance. You're bleeding." I patted around in my bag to retrieve my phone.

"No you're not, Violet." Mama was awfully calm for someone pinned under a golf cart. "Just pick it up. I'll slide out."

"I can't pick it up," I told her.

"I'm not supposed to be out of the house, and if you call the ambulance, I'll be in trouble." How was it that Mama made more sense than I did right now? "If you call the ambulance, they'll make a report, and I'll go back to the clinker. And I'm not betting on Diffy Delk to get me out of this one."

I stopped, took a deep breath, then hit the keys of the phone.

"I told you no!" Mama hollered then groaned.

"Darren," I said into the other end of the phone, "I need your help."

CHAPTER ELEVEN

S mall towns were great. No matter what you needed, someone provided it even when you didn't want them to. In this case, someone called the dispatch, and guess who showed up? Matthew Strickland.

"Why am I not surprised you couldn't stay home?" he asked Millie Kay while the EMTs checked out her noggin and wrapped a huge Ace bandage around her head.

"Is that necessary?" Millie Kay chirped and smacked away an EMT's hand. "And you"—she pointed at Matthew—"you need to find out who did this to me."

"To you?" he questioned then clenched his jaw. He fidgeted as though he were trying to keep his composure. "Is it my fault that you left your house when you were released strictly under house arrest and didn't drive off the curb correctly?"

"Drive off the curb?" Mama spat.

I stood behind Matthew with my mouth wide open, wildly waving my hands for Mama to stop talking.

The whites of her eyes darted past Matthew's shoulder. Being the observant man he was, he twisted his chin and gazed back at me.

"What?" I jerked my arms out of the air and folded them. "Mama's night blind."

"I was on their hides!" Mama shouted. "If it weren't for that dumb curb, I'd probably have run right over them."

"Mama," I gasped, my eye twitching.

"You were chasing someone?" Matthew sucked his cheeks in, and he lifted his hand and pointed to Mama. "Take her into custody," he told the deputy with him.

"Dad..." Darren stepped up.

"Don't, son. There's no amount of explaining why on earth Millie Kay was trying to run someone down after we found strong evidence of her killing someone. We can't have her running around town."

"She wasn't running around town." It was time to come clean, even though I really wanted to collect any clues from the office kitchen. I needed to see if I could pinpoint just who I'd gotten a little too close to in my investigation if they felt like they could break into my office to see what I had.

"That's right. If you aren't going to do your job, someone's got to." Mama wasn't doing herself any favors by refusing to stop talking and let me handle it. "It's bad enough you've got the wrong suspect. Now you're ignoring the breaking into the office where my daughter has all the scoop on the real suspects as the journalist for the *Junction Journal.* After all, she's got Frances's briefcase. There's more clues in there than the little bunny that killed Frances."

"You've got Frances's briefcase?" That was the question Matthew had after Mama told him about the break-in.

Mama was like a freight train. She just kept coming at a barreling speed.

"Did you not open up your ears and hear what I said, Math-ewww?" The usual two-syllable name was drawn out into a few more syllables with Mama's accent to boot. "Someone knows that briefcase contains secrets, and that means they will do anything, like break into the *Junction Journal* office, to get it so they aren't exposed as the real killer."

Okay.

Mama made sense. It got my attention.

Matthews turned around with his hands on his hips, his mouth slightly open, and his tongue fiddling with an edge of his tooth.

"I got a text from your wife saying she didn't see any of the online paper scheduled. I came back to the office to get my laptop so I could work from home to make sure nothing had happened to the paper's online server." Matthew's eyes clouded over when I mentioned the reasons why I went to get the laptop.

I moved on to what he really wanted to hear—what had to do with him and Mama and why she was with me.

"It was late, and I asked Mama to come along," I lied so I could take the blame.

"But—" Mama started to butt in.

"Mama," I said in a stern voice. Darren walked over and sat on the curb next to her, where he politely told her to hush. I continued, "She sat in the golf cart while I went into the office. I'd heard some scuffling in the office kitchen, and I called out, thinking it was Mama. I reminded her that I told her not to leave the golf cart 'cause let's face it, Mama kinda doesn't listen well."

The snicker and grin I expected from Matthew fell short—as in they didn't come at all.

"Anyway, when I went back into the kitchen, someone darted out the door. They ran past Mama, and Mama jumped into the driver's seat. I'm sure her adrenaline took over and blocked out her memory that she wasn't supposed to be out of the house." I placed a hand on my chest. "I take full responsibility for it, and I'm sorry I've not respected the law, but she is right. Someone knows I'm getting close to the investigation, and they either wanted to send me a clear message to stop or that I've got some information that will uncover who Frances Green's killer really is."

The silence was just as heavy as the darkness of the midnight hour. Waiting for my explanation to land on Matthew and allow the space for him to reflect in the moment was almost as excruciating as the urgency I felt to get Mama off the hook.

The scratching sound of sand from underneath Matthew's shoes as he took a step back broke the silence.

"We will go take a look at the office." He turned to the EMT. "Does she need to go to the hospital?"

"Nah. I'm good," Millie Kay insisted.

"She's good. She suffered a scratch to the side of her temple from skidding across the road where the golf cart tipped. There's a small bump, but she doesn't appear to need anything else than to just take it easy." The EMT drew the small pen-type flashlight back into Millie Kay's face and took another look at her eyes. "No concussion."

"That's it. I told you I was fine." She stood up and dusted herself off. "Darren tipped my golf cart back over, and it's got more scratches than me, but I'll be able to drive it home."

Matthew appeared to be going over what she said or what he should do about her. I couldn't tell which, but I knew him well enough to understand that he was able to focus on only one thing at a time.

"Darren, I want you to drive Millie Kay home." The tone of Matthew's voice as he barked orders allowed no room to protest anything he said, so we just did what he instructed. "You, you, and I are going to the office." He pointed at the deputy and me before he opened the back door of his cruiser and gestured for me to enter.

Wanting to be a good citizen and happy to see he didn't haul Mama off back to jail, I got into the cruiser and kept my mouth shut. Later, we were in the office's kitchen, standing by the glass shattered all over the floor.

"Take a look around while we snap some photos and take inventory to see if anything is missing." Matthew made a good suggestion. I jumped at the chance to put some distance between him and me.

My actual office space was the only place in the building that appeared to have been why the intruder broke in, from the looks of all the files thrown to the floor. My laptop and the desktop were still intact, and the cords didn't appear to be tampered with. Or maybe I'd gotten there in time to prevent the intruder from doing damage.

"Anything?" Matthew asked on his way down the hall. He found me standing in the middle of the strewn files. "Don't touch anything." His eyes shifted around the room. "I'll have my team dust for fingerprints and see if we have a match in the system."

He leaned back on the doorframe. I'd seen him do that in different places as he was about to tell me something, so I waited out his silence until he'd formulated what he wanted to say in his head as the words came out of his mouth.

"I think you might be right about the person who broke in here. But I'm not saying it has something to do with Frances's murder. There are many things you have your hand in." He was going into the idea that I was a journalist and uncovered things that weren't meant to be uncovered. "Like the Merry Maker. You've put this huge spotlight on him to get a feature in the newspaper, making the public think you know the Merry Maker's identity."

My lips quivered as I tried not to smile when Matthew referred to the Merry Maker as a he.

"Where is the briefcase? I'd like to have that." He held his hand out.

"It's at my house. When I got it today, I told Emily I would bring it to you, and then I ran into some friends, and my day got away from me, but I'll bring it down first thing in the morning." I put up two fingers as if signifying scout's honor. He gave me a strange look, so I quickly put them down. "Listen, as far as Darren and I…" I was going to inject myself into their tumultuous relationship, though it probably wasn't a good time.

I followed Matthew down the hallway to the kitchen, where the deputies stood at the door.

"I'm finished here. Not much to see." The deputy put the camera back in its bag. "No footprints in the house, but there might be something outside that we won't be able to see until morning."

"Come on," Matthew told me. "I'll have a deputy here all night, so I'll take you on back home and get that briefcase."

I heard the front door of the office open and shut. When I leaned over to look down the hallway, I saw Darren walking toward the kitchen.

"Darren can take me home." I was happy to see my knight in non-shining armor, but he didn't need to know that. He'd come at the right moment.

"Sure. Millie Kay is fine. Your dad got up and said he'd be sure to keep an eye on her and not let her out of the house." Darren might've heard that, but honestly, Mama had her own hold on Daddy. One little wink of her eye made the poor man melt.

"You bring me that briefcase if it's the first thing you do in the morning." Matthew threw a chin to the deputy, using whatever cop language they had between them. The deputy left the office. "I'm still keeping a deputy here," Matthew said. "So let's go."

He was shuffling us out of the cottage, which I didn't want to do, but there was a time to play nice and listen to get what I really needed.

I was the last one out. With my hand on the light switch, I turned the lights off and took one more look back into the office kitchen.

The moonlight pierced the broken glass on the floor, making it glitter. One piece of glass caught my eye. I glanced over my shoulder to see where Matthew and Darren were before I felt I could go unseen to pick up whatever it was grabbing for my attention.

I bent down and reached out underneath the cabinet to the object, careful not to cut myself in case it was a sharp piece of glass.

Immediately, I could feel the smooth surface. When I brought it up to my eyes, I was shocked to see a piece of green sea glass.

That was something I knew I never collected or brought into the office. But someone else did, and I could bet it was the intruder, who never intended to leave this little clue behind.

CHAPTER TWELVE

"Did you hear me?" Matthew asked. He and Darren were waiting for me.

"I'm sorry. I was lost in my thoughts." I slipped the piece of sea glass in my jeans pocket and shut the office door behind me, not bothering to lock it because I hoped the deputy would keep an eye out just in case the intruder realized they'd left behind a little clue.

"What did you say?" I asked and walked around the house with him and Darren.

"I said I'm sorry I interrupted your date this evening." A softness lay in Matthew's tone. "Louise got on me about it, and I'm sorry. I often let work get in the way of my home life, and though I needed to inform the public about the safety issues in the village, I also need to keep what little relationship I have with my son and apologize for interrupting the night."

"Thanks, Dad." Darren put his hand out. "I really appreciate it, but I'm sure I can say that Violet and I only want the safety of the village to be the main priority."

"Speak for yourself," I muttered and dragged my foot in the sand.

"What?" Darren asked. "I couldn't hear you."

"Safety comes first." I nodded, happy his big ears didn't pick up on what I'd said.

"Don't think I didn't see the little whiteboard in your office. That has me thinking someone is on to you, and I should've known you two were snooping around," Matthew let us know.

Dang it. I was really hoping he'd not seen any of that.

"What's up with all the photos?" he asked and noticed Darren and me looking at each other. "If you don't want to tell me, I am more than happy to take the board in for some evidence or possibly see if I can get a tampering-with-evidence charge."

Matthew went from dad mode to chief mode in mere seconds, making it very difficult for me to distinguish between his two sides.

"Will you really listen to our thoughts if we tell you?" I asked.

Matthew leaned on his cruiser and crossed his arms.

"I'm all ears." He heaved in a deep breath.

"Honestly, I can tell you that I don't think my mama poisoned Frances." When he slightly adjusted himself, I continued, "Please just listen and let me tell you about the board. You asked."

"Yeah, Dad." Darren found his voice. "We are more than happy to hear your rebuttal afterwards."

"This isn't some high school debate class," Matthew spouted out. "We aren't at the kitchen table with all that junk."

Obviously, something here needed to be explored as their conversation escalated, but I kept my mouth shut and listened. Like a good reporter.

"We might not be in a courtroom, but we do have some evidence that you should take a look at." I interrupted their little argument. "We collected all the chocolate bunnies Mama had made, even the one she gave Frances."

"We have the one she gave Frances." Matthew seemed very confident.

"Are you sure?" I asked. "Because I have a witness who saw her throw the bunny away on her way from the Incubator to the bunny auditions. I even dug it out of the trash can. I have it at my house."

"And we have the one she gave Diffy Delk on the trolley that morning and the three she gave Goldie Bennett for Joey, Chance, and little Lizzy," Darren said. Matthew's head tilted as his son rattled off their names.

"Mama has the other one she kept for Daddy's Easter basket," I said, rounding out the six.

"Six total." Darren held up his fingers.

"And if you count the candy pieces you took during Mama's house search, you'll be able to count out twelve eyes missing from the 24. Mama has a receipt and the online status of the number of candy eyes she bought from the retailer." I was happy to see he was taking in what we were saying. "I think a good way to check the bunny in Frances's hand is to see if it has the same eyes."

"Which brings us to bullet point one." Darren shoved his hands deep into the front pockets of his jeans. "Did someone from the baking competition want Frances out?"

"Or what about bullet point two, the bunny competition? We did count seven bunny costumes, but only five people—six, counting Frances—should've been in costume. The photo with feet," I reminded Darren. "Which reminds me. Did Owen say I could use his costume?"

"He said he'd bring it in the morning, but we still need to find out who those feet belong to. Plus we have the argument between Frances and Thea. That would round out bullet point three, even though we weren't sure if there were any arguments until Willow told you." Darren and I were so caught up in our own sleuthing that we forgot about Matthew standing there.

"Hello?" Matthew got our attention. "Bunny candy eyes? Bunny toes? Seven instead of six bunnies? Argument with Thea?" Matthew held out his hands and rolled them both, indicating that he wanted us to tell him what we were talking about.

"That's what's on the board," I told him.

"You two found out all of this information in a day?" Matthew asked.

"Has it been a day already?" Matthew looked at his watch, giving a small jab.

"A long one," I said, adding to the flame.

"Fine. Kids." Matthew shook his head.

"Kids?" Darren asked.

"I get it. I get that she's able to get information from people. She's trained to do that. You introduce her to people around here, so naturally people are going to talk to you." Matthew needed an excuse for his big fat ego, but I had to stand where we were. Right now, in order for me to keep sleuthing, I had to stand here and let him believe he was right.

"Are you saying you think there's more than just Mama to consider now?" I asked.

"You've gotten my attention." It was Matthew's little way of telling me he didn't have enough evidence for Mama to be the only suspect. "I need to do my job and consider more possibilities than the one staring us in the face. The poisoned chocolate bunny."

"Yes." I smacked my hands together as the excitement bubbled up in me. "That means Mama isn't under house arrest anymore?"

"That also means we can keep looking into things we think might give us some real answers to why Frances was murdered," Darren stated with confidence that made Matthew squirm a smidgen until he finally agreed.

"Do not put yourself in danger," Matthew said. "Even though I do believe this is a very isolated murder, the facts show there's someone still out there who was capable of killing and could do it again." Matthew pointed at the office. "I can't help but think that person also broke in your office tonight."

I put my hand in my pocket where the secret piece of sea glass was tucked away, determined to find out who had not only tried to frame Mama but had the nerve to break into my office.

CHAPTER THIRTEEN

Darren had convinced Matthew that he would walk me home now that we'd given him reason to believe the killer was still out there. Darren was drawn to the ocean and persuaded me to take a midnight stroll along the beach with our shoes off.

"Not that I want to bring up anything, but I want you to know I heard your father tell you this wasn't a debate team at the kitchen table, something or other." I nudged him to tell me what it was about not because I was being nosey but because the tense reactions in the short exchange between the two men were visible.

My shoes dangled from my fingertips. The waves crashed against the shore, and a breeze fluttered off the sea and rustled the leaves of the palm trees.

"That's just another rung in the ladder my father firmly built between us," he said, referring to the distance between him and his father. "You know how Rhett should've been his son. He was the athlete. The one who only wanted to be the manly man."

There'd been a lot of turmoil between Rhett and Darren, especially after Rhett looked to Matthew as a father.

"Instead of joining the soccer team, I joined the debate team. I was fairly good at it." Darren smiled at the memory. Seeing his genuine smile was so nice. "I found out I was pretty good at overhearing my dad tell Mom about the last court case he had to go to for the prosecution. At the time, I was cutting grass for Diffy Delk."

A hint of Darren's cologne mixed with the familiar smell of the jiggle joint and the salty smell of the ocean.

Every few steps, a little spray of water came off the sea, making us walk a little beyond the break of the waves.

"I would talk to Diffy about Dad's conversations with Mom. I had no idea Diffy was the lawyer of one of Dad's criminals. But Dad was wrong in that case. I would tell Diffy how I was arguing with Dad about the case." Darren's story was all over the place as he jumped between Matthew and Diffy, but I got the gist of it.

"Dad came home after work one day, and it changed our relationship forever." There was pain in his tone. He kept his head straight and looking forward, leaving me unable to see his facial expression.

We found our way past his lighthouse and up the path going toward Holiday Park. In the distance, I could see the glow of the rides from the traveling carnival the Village Council had hired for the Hip Hop Hurray Festival.

"Apparently, this particular criminal was innocent, and what I'd told Diffy, he used in court against my dad. My dad forced me to quit the debate team and told me I couldn't cut Diffy's grass anymore." He snorted. "Then I didn't realize I was my own person and didn't see the grand picture of life. It was like 'these are the rules, and you will live this way.'"

I knew the one reason Darren was opening up to me was because the only light came from the moon and the occasional streetlamp. In the dark, we were most comfortable talking about our shame and secrets, as if the cloak of darkness kept them covered away from the world, away from our hearts, and prevented us from being hurt.

I stopped walking to pretend to take in the view, the peaceful sound of the ocean behind us, and the glow of the carnival lights.

"I'm sorry. That must've hurt you." I had the urge to put my arms around his waist and let the warm feeling of our embrace fulfill his needs at that moment.

We shared a quiet moment, almost a contentment in our solitude, forgetting the chaos of the day.

"I wanted to go to college and become a lawyer. A defense attorney because there were so many criminals Diffy had defended that were innocent. Trust me." He backed away from me. "The criminals who did the crimes certainly deserved to go to jail. When you came to town and started this whole snooping around, making my dad see there was more to the evidence than the surface, I knew I had to hang out with you."

"Oh." I laughed as the truth of why Darren enjoyed being with me became very clear. The grass crunched underneath my bare feet as I walked toward the Holiday Fountain to put my shoes back on. "You are using me to be an adult and stand up to your father because you didn't have the courage to go to college and make a career of something you wanted to do with your life?"

I was feeling a little bit like a weapon Darren was using against his dad.

"I admit I was entertained by you and how you continued to poke holes in all of my dad's investigations, but your strong personality, confidence, kindness, and willingness to do the right thing are making me fall in love with you." He reached out to stop me from walking ahead.

I stopped with my back to him. All of a sudden, time stood still. My soul floated out of my body and burst into the air as though his words were too much for my heart to keep inside.

"Yes. Before you make a big deal out of this, I am falling in love with you, and I wanted to be a defense attorney. You make me stronger." Darren placed his hand on my shoulder, and I turned around.

Looking at him, my eyes teared up, and it was then that I knew.

"I've already fallen for you." The words were a mere whisper as they left my lips, and his lips touched mine.

The killer could've walked right up to us and told us they killed Frances Green, and I didn't think either of us would've given two cares in the world.

At that moment.

CHAPTER FOURTEEN

Night? Sleep? What were those? With a little more hitch in my giddyup, there was no amount of sleep or rest that made me as happy, awake, and alive as the conversation Darren and I had late last night.

Now that I had Darren on my side no matter what, I was ready to tackle my to-do list as soon as I got off work. This morning was a busy one.

I had beat Matthew's secretary to work when I dropped off not only the chocolate bunnies Mama had made but Frances's briefcase with all the files in it. I'd done a thorough check of the files, and nothing stood out to me. The only thing that was of use to me was the ability to take the photos from the files the contestants had sent in while wearing their costumes. I could add those pictures to the ones I'd already taken.

I'd made a few notes and shoved them in my bag to compare to the writing on the whiteboard when I got to work. Then I headed downtown, where I made my first stop of every morning.

Brewing Beans.

"Oh my, someone is glowing," Hazelynn pointed out as soon as I walked inside.

"Maybe it's her bright-orange shirt that's making her olive skin light up and the blond hair giving her a little glow," Hershal said, moving his hands in the air to outline my head as he referred to it.

"Or she got a lead on Frances's murder." Hazelynn got Hershal's attention and mine. "Which is it?"

"Maybe all three." I winked and happily took the coffee they'd started making as soon as they noticed me walking into the coffee shop. "I do have someone who saw Frances having a public fight with one of the bunny contestants. Thea Chase."

"Let me guess." Hazelynn slid me a flat look and raised her brows. "About a bunny."

"I don't know, but they were at the Green Eggs and Honey Rabbit Farm." I was actually most excited about going to check out the rabbitry today.

"Then it was about the rabbit." Hershal tsked and went about making another cup of something green for a customer. "Thea said she was putting her foot down this year."

"Putting her foot down?" I wanted some more clarification on his statement. "Why would Thea do that?"

"Frances's past. She never follows through." Hershal shook his head and handed the customer the drink and pointed her in the direction of the cashier.

I must've looked really confused.

"Thea has that right as the owner of Green Eggs and Honey Rabbit Farm to choose whether or not she sells the rabbits to customers. She's tired of being stuck with the rabbits after Frances decides she doesn't want them or doesn't give them away." Hershal shrugged and plucked one of the order tickets from the machine that spat them out.

"Thea Chase owns the rabbit farm." I saw now that Willow had witnessed the argument because she was there as Maximus Stone's secretary to get the bunnies for his basket.

Frances's basket had those stuffed animal rabbits. It was all making sense now.

"What exactly did Frances do?" I asked and took a sip of the coffee.

"She goes to the rabbitry and picks out three rabbits for her basket during her big debut for the Hip Hop Hurray Festival parade, where she likes to give them out to children. But parents don't want to get a bunny for their children, and they take the bunny back to the farm. Or they refuse it from Frances." A cloud from the steamer rose in the air as Hazelynn made the drink and told me that Frances demanded her money back when the rabbitry didn't give refunds, and the bunnies had no place to go, since no one wanted to purchase bunnies after Easter.

"I'm sure Thea has had her fill of Frances. Frances tried to get her kicked out of the chamber of commerce, and she's the president." Hershal snickered.

The chamber of commerce was like the local government for small business in Holiday Junction. It was much different from the Village Council. Sometimes I'd cover the chamber meetings, which were monthly, if someone good was speaking.

Plus it was a free lunch, and I never liked to give up free food.

"I must've missed that one." I always put the minutes from the meeting the chamber sent over in the *Junction Journal*, but I never recalled hearing about Frances attending a meeting. "Did Frances confront the chamber about Thea?"

"Not that I know of, but I do know Thea is also part of the group wanting to get Frances fired as the head judge. That's all up to the Village Council, though. Which reminds me." Hazelynn rubbed her hands on her apron. "I've got to get started on the cookies for the bunny competition the Village Council is going to judge so we can get an Easter Bunny for tomorrow's afternoon parade."

"The big parade." I snapped a grin on my face, knowing that after today, I'd be swamped with *Junction Journal* obligations, limiting my time to find Frances's real killer. "What time do the cookies have to be at Holiday Park?"

"Eleven a.m." Hazelynn took the apron off and tossed it into what looked like a trash can, but I assumed it was for the cleaning service they used for their aprons, towels, rugs, and anything that needed to be thoroughly sanitized and deep cleaned.

"I have to go down there to take photos. I'll be more than happy to stop by and take them." This way, I had a reason to question some of the Village Council members about Frances and all their claims against her. A great way to get more names to interview.

"That would be such a huge help. Isn't that so nice of her, Hershal?" Hazelynn asked her husband. "I told you southern women will do anything for anyone. Not around here."

"That's me." I chuckled, leaving my true reason for the offer hidden, though I'd still done it without my initial thought. "I'll be here about quarter 'til eleven. Hershal?" I got his attention. "Can I get one coffee to go?"

"For Darren?" he asked.

"Yes, please."

Hershal pointed at me, making it obvious why I was in such a great mood, and my smile grew.

We told each other goodbye, and I decided to walk back down to Holiday Park and take the path down to the beach. There, I'd just walk to the office instead of taking the trolley.

If I was being honest, I was going to avoid Goldie at all costs, since I'd not gotten any more chocolate bunnies for her three grandchildren like I told her I would. Now that Mama wasn't under house arrest, though, I would ask her to make some more.

From what Mama had mentioned before we said our goodnights, she was going to go back to the Incubator this morning because she was still in it to win the baking contest. That would keep her out of my hair for at least a few hours.

If not for Frances's murder looming over the village, you'd never know anything was going on from the already bright, sunny spring day.

The sun would be shining brightly, casting a warm golden glow over everything.

A few fluffy white clouds dotted the blue sky, and the sand was pristine with shades of gold, stretching as far as my eye could see.

People were already on the beach, enjoying the weather, playing games, sunbathing, swimming, and just walking along the shoreline.

Colorful umbrellas were up, and beach towels were spread out all over the sand.

Even the water shimmered turquoise, and the waves were welcoming, lapping gently on the shore.

In the distance, a few boats were out on the water, their sails billowing in the breeze as if there were no cares in the world.

"Good morning." Darren opened the door. His hand grasped the top, and he leaned in. His hair was messy from just getting up. "I like this coffee DoorDash. Is that what I get now that we are an item?"

"An item?" I laughed and returned the kiss he gave me when he leaned down. "I thought it would be great for you to walk me to the office and for us to get a plan together on who we need to go see and why, since my next few days are going to be packed with my real job obligations."

"Mmm." He took a sip of his coffee and hummed. "You even know how I love my Brewing Beans."

"I wish I could take credit, but you're going to have to thank Hershal," I confessed. "Go get dressed, and I'll wait out here. It's too pretty out."

Darren was so fast, I wasn't sure he'd even brushed his teeth until a little bit of peppermint taste lingered after his kiss.

"What's with the grin?" Darren asked as we walked side by side. "I mean, if I'm the reason, I'll take all the credit."

"I was thinking about Hershal and Hazelynn. They both recognized there was something different about me today." I glanced up, and just looking at him made my smile grow even more. "I think they are right. It's you."

"I love that, but this will not let me get anything done that we need to do." He put his arm around me. "We've got to find a way to stop being so happy around each other so we can work."

"Fine," I stated firmly. "But can't we just bask in it for a little bit?" I whined.

"Only until we get to the office." He squeezed me tight as we strolled along the sidewalk and happily sipped on our coffees all the way to the cottage house.

Then we saw the deputy sitting on top of his cruiser.

"How was last night?" Darren asked him.

"Gorgeous. Underneath the stars on a clear night with the sound of the water is magical." He slid off the hood. "Nothing here happened all night. Maybe a sea turtle and a few crabs were seen, but the intruder didn't come back. When the sun came up, your dad, the chief, was here, and we looked for any footprints but nothing. Nothing on the security cameras on the beach poles either."

"What's next?" I asked.

"We've got a big meeting this morning about the festival and the parade. I'm sure the chief is going to assign us a spot on the parade route to keep any eye out, but he said once you got here, I could release the office to you." The deputy looked between Darren and me. "Is there anything I can do before I go? I can do a walkthrough if you want."

"Nah. Thanks, man. We're good." Darren looked down at me for confirmation. "I think the office is fine. My mom will be by later to check out the damages and get Sawyer Dunn here to fix the damages. If you got all the photos and everything you need, I'll clean up while Violet gets to work."

"Yes," I said. "I have to go inside and check the online server to make sure the paper went out as scheduled." Thanks to the recent turn of events, the reason I'd gone to the office in the first place was that Louise had let me know she didn't see the scheduled online version of the *Junction Journal* in the queue.

In all the chaos, I'd forgotten all about it. I had left my laptop in the office again, though it had to stay there for the deputies to collect any evidence. Really, though, I was the one who had collected the little piece of green sea glass.

I'd yet to tell Darren about it. Once we made it inside and were alone, I would.

While Darren cleaned up the pieces of glass and took out the rest of the windowpanes in the old door, I cleaned up my office by picking up all the folders and collecting the papers to put back in the correct files.

By the time we met back up in my office, it was going on ten a.m.

"Knock, knock," Darren said as he entered my office with two coffees in hand. "If we were at my office, I'd be bringing in a few vodkas, but since we are here, this is the best I could do."

"Thank you." I took the mug and turned back to the whiteboard. "I wonder if our intruder saw the board? In any case, I am going to take the cookies the Village Council ordered from Brewing Beans to the bunny tryouts this morning. Did you get the costume for me?"

"Owen is bringing it to the bar in a few minutes. I didn't know it was going to take this much time to clean up, so I'm limited." Darren sat down on the edge of the desk and stared at the whiteboard with his coffee mug in his hands. "I'm going to dress up. I can't let you do it."

"Darren." There was so much power behind the way I said his name.

"No. I won't hear of it. I'll snoop around while you listen, snap photos, and do what you're supposed to do. Besides, Mom wasn't really happy with Dad's suggestion that we ask people about things." He and Louise had already talked this morning.

"That's why she and Marge haven't been down here yet." I thought it was odd they hadn't shown up. "Fine. You're going to be the cutest bunny ever."

"We still have some time." He smiled.

"Darren Strickland." Playfully, I gasped, my jaw dropping.

"What? I don't know what you were thinking, but I was talking about this." He pointed at our investigation board. "We, as the you-know-what, have limited time."

"Oh." I blushed. "Yes. That's what I was thinking." I cleared my throat and placed the last file on top of the desk, where it was before the intruder broke in. "I found something last night the police didn't find."

I dug down into my bag, took the sea glass out, and set it on top of the white desk.

"Sea glass?" He picked it up and held it up to the sunlight shining into the window. "Big deal."

"It's a big deal because I've never had sea glass in here. There's never been a piece of sea glass in this office." I walked over to the board and wrote "sea glass" on it. "I think the intruder had it stuck in the sole of their shoe, and it might have fallen out like shells do, but you and I both know how hard it is to find sea glass, so it's not likely they picked it up on their way here."

"There are a few places that actually sell sea glass." He tossed it in the air before catching it and shaking it in his closed fist. "Green Eggs and Honey Bunny Farm."

"Thea Chase." My eyes lowered as I looked at the board, where I'd stuck the photo I'd taken of her in the bunny costume. "Not only was she trying out for the contest, but she was also trying to get Frances ousted as the judge."

I drew a huge circle around her name.

"Plus Willow saw Thea and Frances arguing at the rabbitry." It still sounded so odd to refer to a rabbit farm as a rabbitry, like a fishery.

I'd learn to expect the unexpected in Holiday Junction. Like they said, "when in Rome," only here it was "when in Holiday Junction."

"Did I hear someone say my name?" Willow popped her head into the office door. She pointed behind her when she saw my reaction. "The door was open."

"Yeah. Yeah. Come on in." I waved her in. "I was just telling Darren about you seeing Thea and Frances arguing at Green Eggs and Honey Bunny Farm."

"Willow, would you like a cup of coffee?" Darren was such a gentleman.

"Thank you, Darren." She smiled and said, "I'd love one."

"I think that's what y'all back home call some good southern manners," Darren said in his best imitation of my accent.

"Don't say 'y'all.'" I shook my head. "It doesn't sound right coming from you."

"What is all this?" Willow walked up to the board.

"It's my investigation into Frances Green's murder." I stood next to it proudly.

"Are you doing one of those big articles like a crime podcast thing?" She leaned in and looked at all the photos.

"Not really. And I know it seems weird, but I have this talent for solving murders," I half joked.

"Then maybe I shouldn't be hanging around you. Bad juju and all." Willow winked. "Just kidding. This is fascinating, but why is Maximus Stone on here?"

"I know he's your boss and all, but as you can see under his name, we listed a motive. Maybe he wasn't going to win this year?" I phrased that as a question, even though it was a real motive. "I mean, it's kinda an ego thing."

I shrugged, finding ways to smooth over the blow of her seeing his name there. Her brows twitched, her upper lip curled, and she showed a little agitation as she picked at her fingers.

"I wasn't going to say anything, but he did tell me he thought he was going to lose out to Nathan Brown." The little bit of information she'd been harboring must have been dying to escape her as she vomited it out. "It's been killing me because I know Mr. Stone is a really good man. He's been great to me and has given me so many opportunities. He is the bunny in so many festivals and so sought-after that if he didn't get the position in his hometown like he'd performed for the last several years, he'd probably lose the other jobs."

"Did he tell you that?" I asked.

"Not in so many words, but he definitely talks about it nonstop. From the time Christmas is over until the day he puts on that suit, it's all he talks about." She frowned. "I can't lie. He told me he'd seen the judging form and wasn't going to win. He's got such a big ego that I don't think he'd do something like hurt someone, but he's a powerful man."

"He saw the form?" I'd been looking for that document, and it was missing from the briefcase.

"Yes." She ran her finger along the coffee handle and then gripped it.

"He didn't tell me who won, but he told me that he'd called Emily at Emily's Treasures to see if she'd gotten any more chocolate Easter bunnies."

"Did she?" I asked.

"Yes. He sent me down there to buy them from her immediately." She gulped. "That was a few days before Frances was murdered."

It made sense. The bunny tryouts had been days apart, and the final was supposed to be the morning when Frances was murdered, but leave it to Frances to have cooked the judges' books and already picked a winner.

"You think Nathan Brown won?" I realized I had no idea about my suspects and really had to get out of this office.

Darren came back in with a mug for Willow and the coffeepot to refill our cups.

"Owen mentioned Nathan." Darren pointed out what Owen had told us at the bar.

"I don't put too much stock in what Owen says a lot of the time." I made more bullet points on the board, listening to what Willow was saying about Maximus.

"Speaking of Owen…" Darren walked over and kissed me. "I've got to go to the bar."

"Yeah. Okay." I nodded because he needed to get the suit from Owen and make it to Holiday Junction in time for the new tryouts.

"Are you two…?" Willow wiggled her finger at me and the space Darren had just occupied before he shot out of the office.

"Exploring it." I turned back to the whiteboard and wrote down "suspect number two" under Maximus's name.

"I didn't say he really did it. I mean, look at Nathan." Her voice held some panic. We had long moved past the kiss between Darren and me.

"Why are you getting so upset?" I asked.

"If Mr. Stone is the killer, what will happen to my job? Me? I just bought my house." She gnawed on the inside of her cheek.

"I'm not saying he did. I'd love to get in front of him. Do you think you could set up a meeting with him?" I asked.

She hesitated.

"Not about this," I said. "I'll make it about an article honoring him for the years he's been doing this. Stroke his ego, like it's all about the goodness of his heart. Yada, yada."

"I guess I could do that." Willow took her phone out of her pocket and typed a quick text.

"What did you say?" I assumed she was texting Maximus Stone.

"I told him the *Junction Journal* wanted to interview him for his service to the village." Her phone chirped. She looked down at the phone, mouthed the words of the text, and smiled. "He said he was at Holiday Park now for the judging and would be more than happy to talk to you now."

"Now?" I jerked to look at the wall clock. "I have to make a pit stop at Brewing Beans first. I told the Hudsons I'd pick up the cookie tray the Village Council ordered."

"Do you need me? I was actually going to the Incubator to finish my bake, since the baking competition is still on." She pointed back at the front door of the office and gathered the items she'd walked in with. "When I was walking past, I noticed the door was open, so I popped in to say hello and thank you for last night."

She picked up the sea glass from the desk.

"Oh, lucky find." Her eyes grew big.

I gathered the things I needed to take to the tryouts so I could represent the *Junction Journal*, snoop, and give Mr. Stone an interview.

"I'll walk with you." I gestured with my head for us to go out the front door. "I didn't find that sea glass. It found me."

"Huh?" Willow questioned.

"Yeah. After you and Pete went home last night, I had to come back to the office, and someone was in here that wasn't supposed to be. They broke in, and they ran off when they heard me. Unfortunately, Mama had come with me and was sitting in the golf cart outside. She went after the person who had run out of the office and had a little golf cart wreck." I frowned and locked the office door behind me. The back door seemed a little more secure now with the temporary fix Darren had made.

"Oh no. Is she okay?" Willow asked.

"Is she? She's great. In fact, I bet you see her at the Incubator when you get there," I said.

We walked down to the sidewalk in front of all the seaside shops, taking a little more time than usual.

I was really enjoying Willow's company. Pete's cuteness didn't hurt, either, though he wasn't with her today. It was hard to move to another town and not know a soul. Willow and I could definitely be friends. Hang out and whatnot.

"I thought she was under house arrest." Willow hadn't heard the news.

"Not that I'm glad someone broke into the office, but they had to be looking for something or know I was getting close to some real answers to who killed Frances, and that made Chief Matthew and me think Mama didn't kill her but was being set up."

Willow audibly gasped when I told her that.

"That's horrible. Who would do such a thing?" She asked the same question people had throughout history, one that would never be answered—why people committed horrendous crimes.

"Your guess is as good as mine, but one of those people on my office board did." I nodded and stopped shy of the Freedom Diner. The Incubator was in the back.

"I'll call you later," Willow said as she took a right down the alley.

"Talk to you then. Thank you for getting me the interview!" I called out to her.

"That's what friends are for!" She made me smile.

Friends.

I loved the sound of that.

CHAPTER FIFTEEN

Holiday Park was filled with so many costumed Easter Bunnies. Everywhere I turned, another six-foot bunny was hopping toward me. It felt like I was in an odd version of *Alice in Wonderland* because some of the bunny costumes literally looked like the White Rabbit from the book.

I stretched my neck and scanned the crowd until I saw Kristine Whitlock and Mayor Paisley standing near the Holiday Fountain.

"Open try-outs have brought out all the rabbits," I said to her and held my camera up. "Let me get a photo of Mayor Paisley."

Mayor Paisley had the cutest set of bunny ears perched on her head. They were white and fluffy on the outside with yellow silk satin lining.

"The yellow goes perfectly with her coloring." I couldn't help but praise how cute our mayor was. Paisley was used to getting her photo taken because as part of her job, she had photo sessions for tourists to get their picture taken with her. After all, it wasn't every day you'd visit a town with a Boston terrier as mayor.

While I snapped her photos and waited for Maximus Stone to show up, Kristine chatted away about Frances's murder and how it hadn't affected the tourist turnout for the Hip Hop Hurray Festival.

"Anything new with the case, other than Matthew coming to his senses and releasing Millie Kay?" Kristine asked just as a bunny with real rabbits in their basket hopped up.

"Hold that thought." My eyes raked up the six-foot-five rabbit, taking in the feet in particular.

"I'm going over to start setting up the Easter-egg-dyeing station." Kristine clicked her tongue, and Paisley jumped to all fours. "I'm so glad you're going to help out there. Come over if you get a chance."

"I'll stop by," I told her then turned to the big tall bunny. "You must be Mr. Stone," I said with some sadness because I immediately noticed the feet definitely didn't have the toes I'd seen in the photo I'd taken before Frances died.

The rabbit nodded.

"Let's go over here." I suggested we move a little bit away from the crowd and that he hop underneath the pink, blue, white, green, and pale-yellow archway of balloons. "I think this would be a great photo."

Maximus Stone knew exactly what he was doing in the costume. Every time I snapped a photo, he'd change positions, which made me smile. He even took one of the bunnies out of the basket and held it out in front of him, making for the cutest photo, which I was definitely going to use in the article.

"How long have you been playing Easter Bunny?" I asked in the interview portion of the line of questioning. Trust needed to be established before I could really dig into the meat of why I wanted to talk to him.

He set the basket of bunnies down. It was intriguing to see how they didn't attempt to get out of the basket. The little pellets of food he put in there had to have helped.

He lifted the head of the bunny costume off and set it on the ground. Sweat plastered strands of his black hair to his head, and his cheeks were rosy.

"I've had the pleasure of working the Hip Hop Hurray Festival for the past fifteen years." He removed a bottle of water from the pants pocket of the bunny costume and took a swig. "It gets really hot in there, but I love it for the kids."

"How did you decide to try out all those years ago?" I asked, finding myself excited to talk to him. It was like I was transported back to my childhood. Awe-inspiring.

"My children were older, and they were beginning to have their family. My wife and I had decided it would be fun to have the Easter Bunny visit after church on Easter. She always had a wonderful Easter brunch." A smile crossed his lips. He lifted the furry arm and dragged it across the sweat on his forehead. "It was a hit. My kids posted photos on the village's social media pages. The next year, the Village Council decided to hold tryouts instead of just sticking someone in a suit."

"I should've researched that." I made a note to go back into the journal archives to see if there was a relevant article there.

"Yeah. I had grandchildren and always tried goofy things to make them smile so I had a good idea of what most kids would like. During the tryouts, I had a mental picture of my grandkids and pretended they were there. I was a shoo-in compared to the ones who just stood there and waved." He pointed his paw at the basket. "Every year, we give our grandchildren a bunny, and so it's a tradition for me to put a couple of bunnies in the basket. When one of the grandchildren comes to see the bunny here at the festival, I give them the bunny."

"That's so cool." I was touched and honored to hear this story. But I knew I had to ask the hard questions. "I also have to ask you about Frances Green."

"Sad, right?" He shook his head.

"Yes, sir, but can I ask you about the initial tryouts before she passed?" I watched as his face stilled.

"Are you referring to the final cuts and me not making it?" he asked.

"Yes, sir. We can keep this part off the record, but you know as the only journalist at the newspaper, I have to cover all happenings in Holiday Junction. I'd love to know if you knew anyone who might want to have harmed Frances."

"Do you mean killed her? Specifically me because I wasn't going to win this year?" He looked down at me and took another drink of his water before he put the bottle back in the bunny pants.

It was fascinating to watch him use the paws to work the water bottle and everything else. It was like second nature to him.

"I'm not going to say I wasn't upset when I got the word I hadn't won. But Nathan Brown has been making his rounds in the bunny circle. He'd done a great job studying me, and he marketed himself really well through social media. He gained a lot of follows, and a few of his videos have gone viral." This was all news to me, but it really did mean Maximus had more motive than I'd initially given thought to. "His social media strategist has really done well. I should get her contact information."

"Nathan has gotten more gigs than just the Hip Hop Hurray Festival?" I asked.

"It's a big business out there. You get all sorts of endorsements. I had one from an Easter candy distributor. They used to send me all sorts of candy to feature on my social media, but this year they decided to go with Nathan." He frowned.

"Big money?" I asked.

"Oh yeah. These companies pay you to promote their products. It's kinda like being a celebrity but in a bunny outfit." One of the real bunnies got a little antsy, and Maximus picked up the basket.

"What will you do now that Nathan has taken over some of your jobs?" I asked.

"My grandkids are older. It's time I hang up the ears if I don't get it today." He seemed to be at peace, more than I thought he'd be.

"What did you do with the chocolate bunnies you purchased from Emily's Treasures?" I asked.

"I gave them to my wife to put in the grandchildren's Easter baskets." He peered down at me. "Are you thinking I gave Frances the poisoned rabbit?"

"I knew you'd gotten some from Emily's Treasures, and the chocolate bunnies seem to be hard to find this year, so someone who'd been able to get a chocolate bunny has to be the killer," I said. "Do you have any comment?"

"Like I said, I bought six. All six are at my house. My wife put them in my grandchildren's baskets. I've already told Chief Strickland, so I'm not the killer." He shrugged his big bunny shoulders. "Listen, I've got to go. Now that Nathan isn't a shoo-in, I just might have one more trick up my bunny sleeve to win this last year."

I had many more questions about this entire bunny gig, but he didn't give me any more of his time. He stuck the costume head back on and hopped away.

Another person in a rabbit costume walked up to me and nudged me, pointing a paw at the camera before doing a little jig.

"You want your photo taken?" I asked and laughed at the rabbit's attempts to get me to turn the camera on them.

The rabbit nodded and put its paws together like it was saying please.

"Okay, only because you seem to have really good manners." I stepped back, put the camera up to my eye, and took a few photos.

The rabbit bowed and walked on by but not without giving me a little swat on the hiney.

"Oh." I jumped, not anticipating that. Then it dawned on me that the rabbit outfit was Owen's. "Darren?" I ran up next to the bunny.

"Yep." He giggled. "Act like you're taking notes so it looks like you're interviewing me. What did Maximus say?"

"He's mesmerizing, really. Super charming. Did you know there's big money to be made as an influencer with companies specifically targeting Easter and the season?" I was still so floored.

"It's no different than any other influencer these days." He hopped and flopped, trying to make sure everyone thought I was doing an interview with him.

"Nathan Brown has this gig in the bag. He has taken the top spot, and some of his videos even went viral. I've not seen them, but that's what Maximus told me. He even has a social media strategist." I was definitely going to look into all of Nathan's profiles. "I wonder what his bunny name is. He's got to have a stage name, right?"

"I guess, but it looks like they are starting." He walked away.

"Hop!" I hollered. He must've heard me because he put his bunny paws up and dropped them down while he hopped over to the line where the tryouts were taking place.

The Village Council members were sitting in almost the exact same spot as the judges before, but the table was much longer.

With my camera lens zoomed in, I made sure I took photos of the judges and got some great snapshots of them laughing when one of the auditionees did something funny. It would be good for the paper to have some candid shots.

When it was Maximus's turn, I focused the camera on him and tried to get some good shots without making them blurry because my hands were bouncing as I laughed. It was cute that he played with the adults like they were children. Now that I understood his process, I could see how he acted out the part and had won so many times.

The Village Council even erupted in applause as he took his bow and hopped off to let the next rabbit go.

Darren.

I shielded my eyes as I watched Darren awkwardly shuffle up to the Village Council. It was almost like he didn't care until he started to do some sort of break dance moves with his arms. He started to hop up to the table and used his furry finger to tap the council members on the heads and tease them, offering them little plastic eggs from his basket and tickling their chins.

He didn't have all the perfect steps and hops like Maximus did, but he was certainly holding his own.

I was so enthralled by him that I realized too late that I'd not gotten any photos of him for the *Junction Journal*.

Matthew Strickland had taken the tryouts very seriously and put deputies all over the park. He was making the safety-of-the-citizens statement he'd made during his press conference a reality.

The line of applicants was so long that the tryouts would take forever, so I decided to walk over to see Kristine at the Easter-Egg-dyeing station.

"It's coming along," I commented to her about the long rectangular table that was going to accommodate multiple people dyeing eggs at once.

The table was covered with a plastic Easter-egg-themed tablecloth, which no doubt would make cleaning up easier.

Bowls of different colors of dye were placed along the length of the table, as were a few of the commercial egg-dyeing kits and food coloring mixes.

"Here, go around with this and add it to the little color tablets in the bowls." She handed me a bottle of vinegar. "I'm going to run and get the hard-boiled eggs."

"What time does this start?" I asked.

"After the parade tomorrow. But I like to get the dye to sit for hours because it really makes the colors more vibrant." She pointed at Paisley. "Do you mind keeping an eye on her?"

"Not at all. I'd love to be of service to the mayor." I looked back at Mayor Paisley. She was sitting with her little black eyes halfway closed as the full sunlight filtered all around her.

I went around the table like Kristine had asked me to and filled up the bowls with the vinegar. The smell reminded me of Easter, when Mama made her famous southern deviled eggs with a touch of vinegar.

"This looks like fun," Curtis Robinson said as he walked up.

"I hope you take a break from the case to come and make an egg." I smiled at him. "How is the autopsy coming along?"

He looked at me.

"I know you can't say much, but I want to offer my condolences," I said. I couldn't believe I said it. "I mean, not that you'd need them, but…" My shoulders fell, and I set the vinegar on the table. "Listen, I know you and Frances had some sort of thing."

"Thing?" His brows rose.

"Look, I'm a journalist, and my eye catches a lot of little things. Little things like a look that's more than just a look. Or an action from, say, a certain coroner who shows up at a scene and covers his eyes when he sees a body that might mean more to him than just a client or case."

He sounded like one of those bulls when they let out a big puff of air.

"Yeah. I guess you could say we were friends. She and I aren't and weren't married, and she's a pretty good baker." He gave half a smile. "It started out when I had repasses at the funeral home. She was bringing cakes and pies for after the service, and once I made a comment on how her pies brightened up the days when I had a really hard job."

It was a bit strange he was opening up to me. Maybe he was comfortable because we were practically strangers who really never talked, but I was all ears.

"She started to bring me something every week that she'd made in the Incubator. She said she was testing things out and wanted my opinion." He laughed. "It was her way of coming to see me. I learned that after a while," he said with a wink.

"I'm sorry for your loss." I picked up my camera and flipped it on. "I took this photo of you, and it touched me." I hit the back button to find it and bring it up on the digital screen.

He leaned in a little closer to see the shot, and then he snorted and nodded.

"It was poison. And not from sleeping medication either." By the way he looked at me, I knew he was talking about Mama. "Iodine poison. It was in her bloodstream, and it's really hard to die from iodine poisoning unless you're given amounts over time."

"Over time?" I questioned. "This means it has to be someone close to her. Someone who she might eat with? Like someone at the Incubator?"

"That's what I thought, too, so I had Matthew get a warrant there last night while no one was in there."

"No wonder he got to Mama's wreck so fast," I muttered and realized Matthew was at the Incubator, probably watching his deputies search the place.

"Millie Kay had a wreck?" Curtis asked.

"She's fine, but someone broke into the paper's office, and Mama was trying to run them down. She would've run over them and gone to jail if the golf cart hadn't turned over her." I tried not to laugh, but

Curtis smiled, and for a moment, he seemed not to be so sad about Frances. "Anyway, I am trying to find out who killed Frances. So if you have anything you can tell me about the autopsy, I'd love to know it."

"I knew she'd been getting this iodine poisoning for a long time because her organs were all messed up. There were traces of iodine in the chocolate bunny," he said. "But not enough to have killed her. When I tested her organs and got the results, I saw this was one of those long-poisoning-type deals."

"That means this was premeditated and could've started a long time ago." This investigation was becoming scarier as more information came out.

The suspect pool just grew beyond the bunnies and even the Hip Hop Hurray Festival.

CHAPTER SIXTEEN

"How's the investigation going, dear?" Mama asked me when I bolted through the door of the Incubator. She had a pan of melted chocolate atop a bunny mold and was carefully filling it up.

"Mama," I scoffed because she was never great at keeping things to herself. Mainly that I was snooping around.

Willow snickered and smiled. She was busy scraping the sides of the mixing bowl to get the batter out into the Bundt pan.

"Everyone here already knows what's going on." Mama shrugged and snapped the identical mold on top so it created a seal with the chocolate-filled mold. She picked the molds up and rolled them all around to create a hollow center. "Besides, they've all asked me about my accident, and I had to tell them why I had refused to stay under house arrest."

Mama was wearing the gauze around her head like a badge of honor.

"You know you can take that off now," I told her. When I looked around, I saw all the same bakers who were there the other day except for Frances. I frowned when I noticed her workstation was empty.

I walked over and stood in her space to get out of the bustling kitchen and wait for Nate Lustig to come back in and check on them.

"How is everyone doing?" I asked and got a lot of grumbles in response.

"We are doing great. Right, gang?" Willow asked in a cheerful voice.

"If you say so," Mama replied and took the little candy pieces for her chocolate bunnies out of her baking box. "How did the auditions go?"

"Great. There were so many people trying out." I threw my voice toward Willow. "Thanks for setting up the interview."

"Interview?" Mama asked.

"Willow got me an interview with Maximus Stone. I can't imagine anyone beating him." It was true. There were so many good candidates, but he had the entire Easter Bunny act down to a wiggle of the cotton tail. "And I don't think he killed Frances," I told Mama and folded my arms.

"I didn't think so, either, but when he bought those chocolate bunnies, I got a little scared." Willow licked the spatula before she stuck it in the sudsy water in the sink. She swirled the dishcloth around and around until the mixing bowl was clean. "Did he help you at all?" She dried the bowl with a dish towel before putting it back on the shelf, where it belonged.

"He did, but I also talked to Curtis Robinson." I was about to tell them what he'd told me, but Nate walked in and asked if everyone was okay in his boisterous voice.

"Tomorrow is the big day, and we have to cool these overnight for them to be ready for all the piping!" he hollered out, giving a slight wave when he saw me. "Do you think you could take some photos while the contestants are baking today and do a little spread about the competition for tomorrow's online edition?"

"Yes. Of course. I've got my camera right here." I lifted the case to show him. "If…" I let the word dangle.

"I've been on the end of one of your ifs before." He was cautious about agreeing to anything, since at one time not so long ago, he was where Mama had been just a few hours previously—on Chief Matthew Strickland's suspect list.

"Let's go into my office and let them bake," he suggested. I put my camera bag on the floor where Frances had worked and used my foot to scoot it underneath the workstation so no one would trip over it.

Nate and I walked out of the Incubator and down the small hall between the working kitchen and the actual diner to his office about midway down the hall.

"I'm telling you we have some really good bakers in this community," he said, like we were doing an interview about the baking competition. Then he sat down.

"I know. That's why I wanted to talk to you, since you and I have been in almost this exact spot." I didn't literally mean sitting in his office, but from the way his brows furrowed, he wasn't understanding what I was getting at. "Frances Green's murder."

"Oh, that." The light bulb went off in his head.

"Curtis Robinson told me Frances came in here a lot more than I realized. I'm not sure if you heard, but she was poisoned." I knew it was a long shot to see if it happened here, but this was a kitchen, an easy place to slip in poison. "I don't think she'd knowingly eat poison. The results of the autopsy show she's been slowly poisoned."

"Slowly?" he asked.

"Yes. Like weeks." I really wasn't sure how long, but weeks sounded good and gave me a pool of bakers that might've come into the Incubator. "How long has Frances been baking in the Incubator?"

"You think we poisoned her?" His words shot out in an offensive tone.

"No. Not you. We have to look at everyone going weeks back to see who might've had enough of an issue with Frances to have killed her," I said. "I know the bakers who use the kitchen bring in their own ingredients, and you allow them to use all the tools."

"That's going to be a lot of people to sift through." He frowned. "She's been teaching classes on the side to make some extra money. I told her it wasn't fair she was in the baking competition, but she insisted she needed the money."

"What about the baking lessons?" I asked, wanting more information.

"We've always offered them, as you know." He opened the desk drawer and thumbed through something until he produced a folder labeled Spring Baking Lessons. "We only let ten people per class sign up because if you get any more than that, it gets a little crowded."

I remembered how cramped it was when Mama and I took the Mother's Day baking class.

"I'm more than happy to give you a list of people in the classes she taught, if you think that'll help." He licked his finger and used it to go through the sheets of class lists and pull out the classes Frances had taught. "There are six classes over the past two months. Is that good?"

"That's more than good. That's great." I knew a lead had to be in there somewhere. "You're the best, Nate."

"Don't thank me yet." He got up and walked over to the copy machine, where he made copies for me. "I can't imagine anyone on this list harming anything but badly baked pie."

"Let's hope not," I said and met him at the copier. He handed me the lists. "I'll keep you posted," I said. "I'll go snap a few photos and put your shout-out first in tomorrow's online paper."

That pleased him as much as a child who got a basket filled with toys on Easter morning. There was so much power in a shout-out in the *Junction Journal*. Now that we'd brought it online, the readership had tripled, which sounded like a lot, but the paper was dying, and we might now have over a couple hundred subscribers online.

From what the local small shops who advertised were telling me and the ad space they were buying up, my plan had been working. It was going to take more time, though.

On my way back to the Incubator to take the photos, I gave the class lists a quick glance.

There it was. The name that hit me in the face.

Thea Chase.

"What was all that about?" Mama asked. "Your face looks funny."

"Gee, Mama, thanks." I laughed and bent down to get my camera bag so I could snap a few action shots of the bakers before I made my next stop.

Green Eggs and Honey Bunny Farm.

"You look like you just heard something important. That's all." Mama stood over me as I bent down. I realized I'd pushed the camera bag back farther than I could reach.

I strained as I reached as far as I could, twisting a little on my side to grab the strap, dragging the bag to me, but it wasn't the only thing I noticed.

"What on earth?" I saw I'd pulled out a dirty apron and picked up both that and the bag as I stood up. "Yuck."

I put the camera bag on the workstation and started to wad the apron up when a photo snap entered my head. A memory of Frances Green standing right here before Mama gave her the chocolate bunny, and Frances had dragged her hands down her apron to clean them off.

I held the apron out and fully open in front of me.

"Oh my." I gulped and saw the chocolate smears. "Frances didn't throw her apron in the cleaning basket."

"Here, I'll do it," Willow offered. "I've got my cake out of the oven and can't do anything with it until tomorrow after it cools completely." She tried to talk like Nate Lustig, making me smile.

"I think I might keep it. Maybe there's something on it." I looked at her.

"Let me get you a bag so you don't mess up anything." Willow hurried off to the pantry and came back with a plastic grocery bag for me to stuff the apron in. "This is exciting," she squealed. She tied up the bag and set it on the workstation. "What are the papers?" she asked as she watched me fold them in half and stick them in the camera bag in exchange for my camera.

"Frances was teaching baking classes, and I can't help but see if anyone on this list could've possibly had a motive to have killed her." I left out the details from Curtis's autopsy because I didn't want the information getting out. It wasn't just Mama and Willow in the Incubator, and maybe one of the people here was on this list.

I kept my mouth shut about the details.

"I do see someone on one of the class lists." I put the camera up to my eye and used my hand to focus in on different bakers perfecting their last attempts at the prize-winning dessert for tomorrow's competition.

"Really? Who?" Mama asked.

"Let's just say that after I take these candids, I'm going to the rabbitry." I clicked away, taking some great shots, though I really wanted to hurry up and get out of there.

It only took about five minutes to get enough photos to pick through so I could get the shots for a quick online shoutout.

"After my visit there, I'll be going back to the office to write the online edition if you want to stop by and help." I directly looked at Mama and shoved the camera back in its bag. I took the plastic bag with the apron in it and pushed it in there beside the camera, but I heard a crinkling noise. Not like the sound plastic would make.

With the apron still in the plastic bag next to my camera, I untied the handles Willow had knotted and patted on the apron. Doing that would leave fingerprints, but I was most interested in Curtis testing the chocolate stains for poison. Careful not to touch the stains, I put my hand in the pocket of the apron and pulled out a piece of paper.

I unfolded it.

Six p.m. private baking lesson reminder.

"Private lessons?" I said in a quiet voice, wondering two things.

Who was Frances Green giving private lessons to, and why would she write it down the morning of her murder right here in the Incubator? The apron she had on was the Incubator's, not hers.

I looked around at all the bakers. None of them seemed to notice me or that I'd found a piece of paper. Quickly, I stuck the piece of paper back in the apron and zipped up the camera bag.

CHAPTER SEVENTEEN

"Do you want to grab something to eat?" Willow asked. "I'm dying for a Diet Coke."

"I love Diet Coke." I walked next to her back down the alley. "But I'm actually going to go to the Green Eggs and Honey Bunny Farm before I have to go back to work and upload all the photos." I nudged her a little. "I got some really good ones of you that are definitely going in."

"Do you want company?" she offered.

"Sure." It was so much better when someone went with me. That way, it didn't look like I was there to snoop. "And you know Thea, so it won't seem apparent why I'm really there."

I patted the camera bag.

"You're going to get an interview?" Willow asked.

"No. I was going to use that angle because it works wonders on getting in the door to snoop without anyone really knowing I'm doing it." I winked.

The ding of the trolley echoed, telling us it was coming before we'd even seen it.

"Let me run in the Freedom Diner and grab a Diet Coke." She handed me her baking box and hurried inside the diner.

Holding her stuff and mine made it difficult for me to answer the phone ringing deep down in my bag. I bent down, put our stuff on the sidewalk, dug deep in my bag, and retrieved the phone.

"*Junction Journal*," I teased Darren, who was on the other end. "Can I get an interview about the most eligible bachelor in Holiday Junction being taken off the list?"

"Yes, but you can also add that the most ineligible bachelor is also the newest"—I was preparing to hear him say "Merry Maker"—"Holiday Junction Easter Bunny."

"What?" Goldie Bennett could've jumped the curb with the trolley and hit me, and it wouldn't've surprised me more than his news.

"Yeah." He cackled in disbelief. "Crazy ,right?"

"I'm shocked." I looked to see who was touching my arm.

It was Willow's elbow as she double fisted two Diet Cokes, pushing one out to me. I tucked my phone between my ear and my shoulder, whispering "thank you" as I took the soda.

"That's amazing," I said just as the trolley dinged.

"What are you doing?" he asked. "I was on my way to the office to see you."

"I'm going to go to Green Eggs and Honey Bunny Farm to talk to Thea, but you can meet me back there in about an hour." I took a step back from the curb as the trolley barreled down the road.

It looked like Goldie wasn't going to stop the darn thing, but she was good at stopping right on a dime. She made a perfect landing every time, and this time was no different.

The folding door of the trolley swung open. Goldie was leaning over the handle and chomping on her gum. The bunny-ear headband and the plastic bunny nose held on by a string of elastic around her head completed her choice of outfit today.

"You coming?" she asked.

I nodded and gestured for Willow to board before me while I finished my conversation with Darren.

"I'll see you in about an hour." He sounded giddy, and I knew it wasn't because of me. It was because he'd just scored one of the most beloved volunteer positions you could get at the Hip Hop Hurray Festival.

"Green Eggs and Honey Bunny Farm, huh?" Goldie jerked the door shut as soon as my foot landed on the top step inside the trolley. "Did you get my chocolate bunnies?"

"They aren't ready yet. I was just at the Incubator, and she was making a fresh batch. Right, Willow?" I wanted Willow to back me up.

"Yep. That's right." She saved me a spot on the bench behind Goldie. No one ever wanted to sit behind the driver. "What's that about?"

"When Mama was a suspect, she'd given out all the bunnies she'd made at the Incubator, and I went around to collect all the chocolate bunnies so Curtis could test them for poison and prove Mama didn't kill Frances," I whispered. I put my bag and camera bag on the floor between my feet as I sipped on my Diet Coke. "Mama gave Goldie three for her grandchildren. Luckily, I was able to collect all six of them, even the one Mama had given Frances when Frances left the Incubator that morning."

Willow's brows rose, and her mouth dropped open.

"How did you get that back?" she asked. "I thought it was in her hand when she died."

"That was what everyone thought until someone told me they'd seen Frances throw it in one of the trash cans along the ocean." I laughed, trying not to snort Diet Coke out of my nose. "You should've seen me digging through the trash. Nasty," I snarled.

"My goodness. Millie Kay is lucky to have you." Willow smiled and held her Diet Coke can up to me, clinking mine for a Diet Coke toast. "I'm lucky to have you too."

"You know, I was thinking the same thing about you. It's nice to actually have a friend here." I felt an inner warmth, the kind you feel when you meet a new friend and immediately know you've got a lot in common.

It would be fun to watch our friendship unfold, and I was really looking forward to it.

"I'm really glad you're coming with me. Thank you for the Diet

Coke." I wanted to make sure she knew I appreciated her and her kindness.

"That's what friends are for." She handed me her can, leaned on her hip, and got her phone. "Maximus Stone." She showed me the screen and slightly turned to take the call.

She put her finger in her ear and bent her head down, something I probably would've had to do to hear over the old trolley's clacking and the chatter around us.

Her conversation lasted the entire fifteen-minute ride and continued after we'd gotten off the trolley.

"I'll bring you some of those bunnies," I told Goldie. When I got off the trolley, I found that Willow had stepped away.

A cute wooden sign at the entrance read Bunny in Blooms and listed the dates of spring. This was just another example of the treasures I'd yet to really explore outside of Holiday Junction's village limits.

Another sign, one with a trash can next to it, also read that no outside food or drink was allowed in the rabbitry for the safety of the bunnies. Only one sip was left in the soda can, and from what I remembered people telling me, it must have been the gathered-spit sip, so I tossed the can.

The rabbitry was much different than I'd initially thought it would be. There were several A-frame-type structures with wire around them as well as a bigger pen with several smaller wooden houses and climbing structures for the little rabbits.

"Isn't it cute?" Willow's call had ended. She found me inside, where many little kids were running around with bunnies in their arms, trying to plead with their parents to buy them a furry friend. "You should get one. You don't have a pet, do you?"

"No thank you," I politely declined. "I only have time to take care of Mama. It wouldn't be fair to the bunny for me to be gone all the time or have to be at Mama's every whim. Mama is a full-time job."

Being a southern woman's daughter involved a lot. It was a full-time job in itself and kept me on my toes more than running the *Junction Journal*.

"Speaking of jobs, time to play the part." I swung the camera bag around to my chest and unzipped the bag to get the camera out. The lists of clients from Frances's baking lesson Nate had photocopied for me fell out.

"I got it." Willow bent down and picked it up. "What's this?"

"Did you know Frances was giving private baking lessons?" I asked Willow.

"No. Really?" Her brows furrowed. "Can I take a look?"

"Yeah. If you see someone on there besides Thea Chase that might've had a little beef with Frances, let me know."

The door of the blue shed-style building popped open, and a woman with hair slicked back into a bun, thick black glasses halfway down her nose, and a bunny-patterned dress with green-and-white-striped leggings tucked into a pair of muck boots walked out.

"Is that Thea Chase?" I asked Willow, since I'd never seen the lady outside the bunny costume. Frances's file didn't have before and after photos like all the others did.

"Yep. Hey, Thea!" Willow looked up from the class lists and handed it back to me, folded.

I stuffed the papers back down into the front pocket of the camera bag and followed Willow. We met Thea halfway.

"This is Violet Rhinehammer from the *Junction Journal*." Willow immediately began the introductions. "She saw Maximus with the bunnies at the tryouts, and I told her about your farm."

"Yes. I was telling Willow how much I wanted to come out and get some photos of the bunnies for the online paper—and give the rabbitry a plug." I wagged the camera.

"We have the perfect Holland for this." Instantly, her face glowed with excitement as she hurried us over to one of the pens.

No wonder she had on muck boots. Her feet sank in all the shavings and coverings at the bottoms of the pens when she stepped over the wire fence and picked up the cutest grey-and-white bunny.

"This is Blue Belle." Thea lifted Blue Belle up to her chest and immediately began to snuggle her, something I didn't see a killer doing.

Doubts that Thea had killed Frances started to creep up the more she talked about her passion.

The bunnies.

"She's a Blue-Fawn Harlequin Holland Lop. She is female. She is very interested in everything and loves to be petted." Thea uncurled the rabbit from her chest and gently held her out to me. "Would you like to hold her?"

"No. I'm good." I shook my head, but Willow wouldn't hear of it. She grabbed my items. "Um-kay." I laughed and took the rabbit.

"Closer," Thea encouraged me. "Blue Belle likes to snuggle." After I correctly moved into a holding position, Thea grinned. "You're a natural, and Blue Belle is looking for a home."

"I was telling Violet that she needs a pet. Pete is so much company to me, and of course I can't have a bunny, though they are so cute," Willow squealed and bent down to look Blue Belle in the face, giving me the perfect opportunity to shove the animal into her arms as I took back my things.

"Though I do think Blue Belle is adorable, I'd love to get a few photos of you with her." I busied myself with switching on all the camera features. I was going to use the automatic mode since I was really here for other reasons and didn't bother to do any photo details.

Shoot and click.

"These are great." Willow stood behind me while the camera clicked away, and the photos came up on the digital frame.

"They really are." I was shocked to see that when Thea sat down, Blue Belle hopped right into her lap. "She's a natural for the camera."

"She's a star," Thea trilled.

"Speaking of stars, can you answer a few questions about the Easter Bunny tryouts?" I shoved the question in there, continuing to take photos and move around to get all different angles and other bunnies in the photos.

"I was excited to try out this year. It was the first time I tried out, but I knew it was a long shot." I zoomed the camera in on her face as she talked. Her demeanor had definitely changed. She took Blue Belle out of her lap and set her back in the pen. Thea began to brush herself off.

"Why was it a long shot?" I asked. "I thought your costume was great."

"It was, wasn't it?" She smiled. "That was a very old costume my daddy used when I was a kid."

She gave me a gentle reminder that holidays went back generations here in Holiday Junction. Memories at every season made life so bitter-sweet for them.

The fond memory of her father and the ability to use the costume for good showed on her face. Again, that was something I didn't see a killer doing.

"First year? Wow." I thought about her and how I just didn't think she killed Frances, but I knew I could ask her about the bunny feet to see her reaction. "Can I show you something?"

"Sure." She nodded and leaned in when she realized I was going to show her a photo on the camera.

"I'm sorry, but I have to come clean. My mama is Millie Kay Rhine-hammer, and when she was Chief Strickland's number-one suspect in Frances Green's murder, I used my skills as a reporter to find things out."

At the sound of my words, she pulled away from me. She looked at me with a frown on her face.

"I heard you and Frances had gotten into a pretty big argument. Can you tell me about that?" I was happy she allowed me to finish my question and didn't kick me out of the rabbitry.

"I did. I was tired of her buying my precious bunnies only to bring them back. They might just be bunnies, but they know when they aren't wanted. I refused to let her do that again. That was why I didn't get the Easter Bunny job. She had a motive to kill me, not the other way around." She was really willing to tell her side. "I told Matthew Strick-land that, too, when they asked us for a statement at the crime scene. He also asked if they could search the rabbitry and my home for some-thing, I guessed for whatever they thought killed her. Of course, I don't keep anything in my home or here that's not safe for all animals. Everything is organic."

"No wonder he didn't have you as a suspect." I smiled, wishing I had some sort of contact in the police department so I didn't chase dead ends. If I'd known Matthew had already cleared Thea, I would've moved on to Nathan Brown.

As a last attempt to find out the killer and since I was there, I dug down in my bag and pulled out the piece of sea glass. "Also, I understand you collect sea glass and sell it."

"Yes, among other things, like eggs, chicks, and some of the clay pieces I've made at Ceramic Celebrations. We love that place." She pointed at the shed, which must've been the rabbitry office.

"It's so much fun," Willow followed up. "We should do one of those sip-and-clay classes they offer where we can sip on wine and make something cool. I've always wanted to do one of those."

A warm fuzziness arose in my soul when Willow suggested the class. I was finally getting settled in Holiday Junction with a relationship with Darren and an exciting new friendship with Willow.

If I could only solve this darn murder.

"Would you like to purchase any?" Thea asked, bringing me back down to earth.

"Chicks, no, but I'd love to see your sea glass collection," Willow said. "Sea glass is really hard to find. I've never found any. I've looked too."

"The truth of the matter is someone broke into my office, and I can't help but think they knew I was getting close to the killer, though I have no clue. I found this piece of sea glass on the floor left behind by the intruder." I held it out for them to see.

"Do you think they left it there on purpose?" Willow asked. "I've seen those crime shows where the killer leaves something behind."

"That's true." Thea nodded and picked it up to look at it. "It's been cleaned." She held it up to the sunlight.

"Sea glass has to be cleaned?" I knew nothing about sea glass, but it was definitely something I would research when I got back to the office.

"Yes. Cleaning makes it really shine." She handed the piece back to me. "I'll show you mine."

"I was thinking the killer had walked on the beach and gotten a piece of sea glass in the groove of a shoe, but now that you say it's been cleaned, it makes me wonder if the killer collects sea glass."

Willow shivered. "The thought is awful," she snarled and walked ahead of me to follow Thea into the office.

The shed was much larger than I'd anticipated.

Inside were big brown woven grass buckets filled with eggs of various shades of brown, blue, and cream. They weren't like the ones you saw in the grocery store.

"I'll definitely take two dozen eggs." I could taste my mother's cooking before I said, "Millie Kay makes the best egg salad for Easter brunch that'll knock your socks off."

"She's a doll." Thea got an empty egg carton from a stack and walked over to fill up two of them. "The sea glass is over there."

Willow and I went over to the wooden stand, which held several clay pots I was sure Thea had made with her own hands from Ceramic Celebrations, the local pottery shop. Each bowl had a different colored sea glass in it, but none looked to be the same shade of green as the nearly teal piece left behind by the intruder.

"I don't see a match, do you?" I asked Willow. Both of us glanced one more time, holding the piece I had up to some that we thought could match.

"No. I'm sorry." She frowned and put a hand on my shoulder. "I can ask around to see if anyone collects sea glass."

"You're going to be checking everyone in Holiday Junction," Thea said. "Practically everyone came here for Easter to get not only a bunny but some sea glass for Easter centerpieces. They do make beautiful tablescapes with freshly cut flowers."

After I paid for my eggs, I asked Thea, "Do you mind looking at the photo I wanted to show you?"

"I'd love to." She came back around and leaned again, making room this time for Willow to see.

"When I was at the initial tryouts…" I was trying to tell her how I'd gotten the photo.

"You mean the one where Frances had already picked Nathan Brown to win?" she asked.

I guessed it was a big secret that really wasn't a secret.

"Yes. Though I had no idea, and Mama wanted me to take her photo while she was at the judges' table." I was going to tell them how excited Mama was that she'd been asked to judge, but we'd been there for about forty minutes, and I had to get back to the office.

My new boyfriend was going to be there. My heart fluttered when I thought about it.

"Anyway, I took this photo." I showed them.

"She's so darn cute," Willow said, and Thea agreed.

"Look at the table." I used the plus button on the camera to enlarge the photo. "See, there's a bunny foot in the photo and a faint paw where it looks like someone put a chocolate bunny on the table. The chocolate bunny that had some of the poison in it, which was in Frances's grip."

"My goodness. I see it." Willow grabbed Thea and jerked up to look at me. "Who had on that costume?"

"I don't know. That's the problem. I have the accounted six bunnies but not the seventh." I could see Thea counting the participants in her head.

"There were five contestants—six with Frances dressed up." Thea snapped her fingers. "You're right. Who on earth was there? And in this costume?"

"I thought you might know. It doesn't match any of the contestants." I quickly flipped through the photos I'd taken.

"There's the winner." She pointed at Nathan. "Maximus got robbed. I knew I was a long shot, but honestly, Maximus does a great job." She turned to Willow.

"Nathan didn't win." A look of shock crossed Thea's face but not Willow's.

"I heard it was Darren Strickland." Willow gave a wry smile. "That's what the phone call was about from Mr. Stone."

"I'm sorry, Willow. I bet he's very upset, but at least Darren won. Wouldn't Frances die?" Thea tucked her lips in. "I mean, if she were alive."

"I knew what you meant." I put the camera back in the bag and took my eggs. "I got some great photos to put in tomorrow's online article about the festival, which is why I've got to go and do that."

Willow's phone rang again. She hurried out of the shed.

"I think she's being called to work." I followed her out, and Thea walked out with me.

"You know, my family has a huge history of bunnies and bunny costumes. If you want to send me the photo, I'm more than happy to try to track down the years that costume was made," Thea offered. I accepted.

While Willow took the phone call, I went ahead and got my camera back out. I used the rabbitry's Wi-Fi to send the digital photo directly to Thea's phone.

Gotta love technology.

"I've got to get back to town," Willow called and pointed at the trolley driving around the bunny farm's parking lot.

"I'll come!" I yelled after her as she started to jog out of the rabbitry.

It took a minute for me to catch my breath once I got back on the trolley. Willow was sitting on the same bench.

She was eerily silent.

Once we sat there for five minutes without speaking, I asked, "Are you okay?" Though the clacking of the trolley and the chatter of the passengers made the ride far from quiet, we were silent with each other.

"You know that phone call I just got?" she asked. The lines between her eyes deepened. "That was Mr. Stone. He said something about him and his wife leaving town for a while, and he wants to see me now. I think I'm getting fired."

"Fired?" I asked.

Slowly she nodded.

"You know those papers that fell out of your camera bag?" She looked down to where I'd put the camera bag back between my feet on the floor of the trolley.

"Yeah. The class list of Frances's baking lessons," I confirmed.

"I can't believe I'm saying this, but Sandy Stone was on two of the lesson sheets." Willow gazed down, unable to look at me.

"What are you saying, Willow?" I asked.

"I think she might've killed Frances Green." She gulped back her tears.

CHAPTER EIGHTEEN

Willow was so visibly shaken up that she stayed on the trolley. She said she wanted to go home and let Pete out before she went to the office to be fired.

I tried to assure her that even if she did get fired, whatever was happening with Maximus and Sandy Stone didn't have anything to do with her job, but she was so busy crying that she blubbered something about the company and her being the secretary that I couldn't understand.

Before I got off the stop near the office, I told Willow to call me if she needed me. That was what friends were for.

"Mama?" I called when I walked in and smelled coffee. She was always brewing a pot.

"Just made some coffee!" She confirmed what I already knew and peeked around the kitchen door down the hall. "I've got those bunnies for Goldie's grandkids. What did you find out about Frances at the rabbitry?"

She hurried into the room with a tea tray that bore two mugs and the coffee carafe.

"Thea didn't do it, and she already gave her statement to Matthew Strickland." I walked over and hugged Mama before I made my way to the whiteboard. I needed to write down that Matthew had already cleared Thea and that the police had searched her home and business and found nothing, or else she'd have gone to jail.

"You don't know anyone in the police station who'd have a little insider info, do you?" Since I moved here, it'd proven hard for me to uncover people's secrets. It wasn't like home, where I grew up with all the folks and people my age were now in roles that allowed me to gain information.

Not here.

"Now why on earth would I know anyone?" She stood next to me, eyeballing the whiteboard, and shoved a mug in my hand. "Here, coffee will help rev up that smart brain of yours. You'll figure it out. I have no doubt. You always do."

Mama was always my cheerleader, even in situations that looked bleak or impossible.

"Now. I've got to go. Things to do before the Bake-Off tomorrow." Mama stood at the door. She didn't bother making herself a coffee. "Do you need anything else?"

"Yes." I snapped the lid back on the dry-erase marker. "Did you know Frances was giving baking lessons? Possibly private ones?"

"She did talk openly about it during times we were at the Incubator. She and Nate, that is." Mama's eyes narrowed. "You think someone at the Incubator killed her?"

"I did find out from Curtis Robinson that Frances had been poisoned slowly with iodine. Like over a span of days, maybe longer."

"See. That's why I don't taste nothing other bakers ask me to while I'm there. I politely tell them my palate is southern, and my taste buds wouldn't make me an honest judge." She nodded. "I always refer them to Nate. And he hasn't gotten sick."

She made a good point, which again led me to believe it had to be these private lessons—and back to the person Willow pointed out. Maximus Stone's wife, Sandy.

The big question was why Sandy would want to murder Frances.

"Well, if you don't need anything, I've got to go. The bunnies aren't going to glue their eyes on themselves." She snorted at her own joke. Such a Mama thing to do.

"By the way, Matthew Strickland stopped by to talk to you. He asked me to have you call him."

"Did he say what he wanted?" I asked.

"He came in here, looked at your board, and said all the people you had on there had been cleared, even me." She shrugged and then said, "I also went ahead and got online to post all of the events, so you just have to upload all the photos you've taken from the bunny tryouts, the Incubator, and, I'm guessing, the Green Egg and Bunny Rabbitry."

Really? I looked at her as questions swirled in my head about why she'd not started off the conversation with all this information when I walked through the office door. It would've certainly saved me the time it took to write down all the things about Thea.

"Well, I think I'll catch the trolley home after I put the candy pieces on my bunnies. My golf cart isn't back from the shop, and I'll just give Goldie her three. Plus I made a special one for Diffy." She walked across the hall to her office.

I sat at my desk and moved the mouse to bring the computer monitor to life. Getting on the server for the online paper was much easier than using my laptop.

"There's our bunny!" Mama squealed when she noticed Darren walking up to the office. She rushed to the door and swung it open, bringing a warm breeze that fluttered off the ocean with a hint of sea salt into the office. "I'm so proud of you," she chirped when Darren walked inside.

She put her hands on each side of his face.

"You are going to be a fabulous bunny. They loved the dance moves the most, and that's what the council remembers." Mama beamed with pride as though Darren was her child.

"Thank you, Millie Kay." Darren broke out into the arm wave as she clapped in delight.

"I've got to go." Mama turned back to me. "I'll see you at home later tonight."

"Bye," I said, waving at her. Then I walked over to Darren and wrapped my arms around him. "Congratulations."

"Thank you." He kissed the tip of my nose. "But I couldn't wait to come see you. Do you feel this?"

He pulled back a little and gestured between us.

"It's weird, right?" I knew the entire situation was odd. "We go from butting heads to almost dating to flirting and near kisses to this."

"Are you good with it?" he asked.

"Does it look like it?" I quickly pulled away when I heard the office door open. "Mama, you forget something?"

I walked to the door and looked into the hallway, where Matthew Strickland was standing.

"Hey, Darren is here." I nervously pointed behind me and had no idea why I would say that. "I was about to return your call."

"Actually, I was down at the Incubator, talking to Nate again, and on my way home for the day when I decided to stop in." He walked with me into the office, greeting Darren with a hard nod. "Did Millie Kay tell you about your suspects here?"

"She did. We gave it a shot." I shrugged. "I did want to show you this. Or maybe Nate did."

I wasn't sure what Nate and Matthew had talked about, but as long as I had the class list from Frances's private lessons, I might as well give it to him.

Matthew stared at me.

"What? If I can't help snoop around anymore, we might want to know everything I've found out." I pulled the list out of the camera bag. "I've not even had time to show Darren."

I ran my finger along the crease of the folded pages and handed them to Matthew. He and Darren stood shoulder to shoulder. The resemblance was uncanny. Darren was more like his father than he'd care to admit.

"That's a list of Frances's students in her baking lessons. It seems to me that it's not a coincidence that Maximus Stone's wife, Sandy, is on there twice. Once last October and November and another one in

December." I couldn't help but curl my mind back to fond memories of those times. "And if you look at the upcoming class schedule, she's signed up for a couple more in the future."

Mama had bought her house, Dad moved here, and we had our first Christmas together in a cute and cozy town. Gratitude filled me.

"Also, I was with Willow Johnson, Maximus's secretary. She thinks she's getting fired. Apparently, Maximus does a lot of bunny appearances and has all this income from influencers." I watched them as they started to digest the severity of the situation.

"And if he isn't getting jobs, the influencers will have no problem going after the hot rabbit." Darren got it.

"Trust me, I know when you take money away from a wife, it can get pretty dicey." Matthew smiled. He was half joking but then said, "If it weren't for this paper, I'm sure your mom would be more up in my business and spending more money."

"Chief Strickland," I said formally, "is this your way of complimenting me for saving the *Junction Journal*?"

"Yes, it is," he said. It was nice to see him soften a little, especially around Darren.

"I'm guessing you know about the iodine?" I asked and saw the surprised look in Matthew's eyes. It seemed he didn't know that Curtis had given me the little piece of information.

"You're thinking Sandy has been somehow slowly slipping the iodine in the food?" he asked.

"I'm not sure how Frances ran her cooking lessons, but if she mimicked them at Nate's Incubator, he was the only one who would taste test what was being made." I was saying Sandy had the opportunity to slowly poison Frances without anyone ever knowing. "Did you test the bunny?"

"Yes. It had poison in it but in small trace amounts." Matthew confirmed what I'd feared.

"We do have this." Darren walked over to the board, pulled out the photo of Mama sitting at the judges' table, and handed it to Matthew. "You can see a bunny foot there and the chocolate bunny being put on the table. This bunny is not one of the six that were supposed to be in costume."

Darren went on to show Matthew all the photos of the costumed citizens to prove that the seventh bunny could very well be our killer.

"It looks like I need to get a warrant for the Stones and see if we can find any iodine and bunny costumes with feet that look like this." Matthew was open to what Darren and I had found out. "Now that is your last bit of investigation, right?" His brows rose, and he looked at us from under them.

He looked down at his utility belt, where his phone had chirped.

"That's your mom. She said dinner is ready." He held the photos and the baking class list in his hands. "Can I keep these?"

"Sure. Anything you need if it'll help." I felt a sense of relief he had listened to us.

"Do you two want to come eat?" Matthew offered.

"I can't, but you go," I encouraged Darren. He and his dad seemed to have some sort of connection at the moment, and I needed to capitalize on it.

I wanted to make it my mission for those two to get closer than they were. Darren hadn't yet realized just how precious life was and how fast it went by. Not to mention that in the blink of an eye, life could change.

"Sure. I'll go get my scooter and come on over." Darren accepted his dad's offer.

"We'll see you soon then." There was sincerity in Matthew's tone. I walked him and Darren to the front office door. Matthew turned back and said, "Congratulations on the Easter Bunny gig." He wiggled his nose and then headed out the door.

Darren and I laughed. His genuine laughter sounded like music to my ears.

"Are you going to be okay here?" Darren asked.

"I'm actually going to put the schedule on tomorrow's paper and head on home to check on Mama. I need some sleep." I waited to see if he was going to kiss me goodbye. It was clear I'd been making all the first moves, and I wanted him to do it this time.

"This bunny has an early wakeup call. He's got to be at the parade bright and early." He pulled his shoulders up to his ears and put his hands out. "The star of the show has to get as much sleep as he can."

He wrapped his arms around me and tugged me closer to him.

"How do you feel about the co-Merry Maker also being the most popular bunny for Easter? Can you handle all my fame?" he teased and winked, sending my heart into its own hip-hopping.

"You can have all the limelight. Just as long as you don't hop away from me." I loved using all the bunny references. They made me giggle when the darkness was still around us.

"We need some light shed on a holiday that should have the spot-light on it." Darren was showing his sentimental side, which was how I knew he was opening up to me. "Are you sure you don't want me to wait and take you home?"

"No. I'm good." I gave him a kiss. As he walked away, a little bit of my heart trailed behind him. I'd always been told never to watch someone leave because it was bad luck, but he had too good a back view for me to drag my eyes off him.

CHAPTER NINETEEN

For a moment, I regretted not taking Darren up on his offer to see me home. The silence of the office and the ocean breeze that picked up during high tide made the old cottage groan and come to life in an unnerving way.

I couldn't wait for Sawyer Dunn, the local contractor, to finish with his current project so he could get the kitchen door truly fixed. Plus I wanted him to put bolts on the door.

"There you go." I hit the schedule button and the desktop's off button and put the laptop in the office drawer.

Tomorrow was going to be an off day for the *Junction Journal* office. As an employee, I'd be taking photos of the parade and the cutest Easter Bunny ever before I had to help with the egg-dyeing station.

I couldn't get out of the office quickly enough and was just in time to catch the trolley.

"You're lucky you got me. Last stop." Goldie looked like a tired bunny. Her perky ear headband had turned into a choker with the ears sticking out the back. "I'm exhausted by the end of the day. You should've gotten the last ride. I took your mama home, and she gave me the three bunnies for little Lizzy, Chance, and Joey."

"You be sure to bring them to dye eggs tomorrow after lunch, because I'm going to be working it, and I'd love to see them." I sat right behind her, even though the entire trolley was empty. "And I'll take some photos of them for the paper."

"Oh, their mother will die if they make the paper." Goldie was so excited to imagine the joy that would bring her daughter. It was Goldie who would buy up every single print copy and even put one on the visor of the trolley.

She wasn't fooling me. I loved making people happy, and this was a little way to do that.

"You're a good friend to Willow." Goldie was referring to the earlier situation in which Willow was sad. "She talked about how grateful she was for you then broke down in tears."

"Oh no." I felt bad that I hadn't texted her to check on her. I moved the camera bag and picked up my handbag to get my phone out. "I need to check on her. I wouldn't be a good friend if I didn't."

"We will be passing by her house." In no uncertain terms, Goldie suggested I pop in to see her. "I've got an extra chocolate bunny I was going to give Elvin, but he don't need it. He's got sugar anyway."

I laughed, wondering why on earth she'd give her husband the sugary treat if he was a diabetic, but that was something I didn't need to know.

"I think you're telling me I need to check on her." I looked at her reflection in the mirror near her head, the one she used to look back at the passengers. "Fine. Make my stop there, and I can walk home."

"A few minutes won't hurt. She was pretty upset." Goldie didn't mention if she knew why, but she was sure Willow was upset and needed a friend.

"In Willow's own words, that's what friends are for." I knew it was the right thing to do. Something told me.

Goldie didn't say any more about it on the way there. She made chitchat about her grandchildren and where they were going to stand for the parade. It was one of the things the children loved almost as much as they loved the Easter Bunny.

"Here we are." Goldie stopped the trolley in front of a small home where the siding was falling off. One of the shutters was cockeyed next to the window.

"Is this Willow Johnson's house?" I asked.

"Um-hmm." Goldie shoved the lever to open the door. "You're a good friend."

It was Goldie's odd way of telling me without telling me not to judge Willow and where she lived.

"Thanks." I gathered my belongings and took the chocolate bunny from her before I got off. I didn't bother looking back when I heard her jerk the trolley's folding door closed and zoom off.

I hadn't been to this neighborhood before, and it didn't look like there was much life there.

I knocked on the door and heard footsteps coming before I saw a shadow peep out the small window next to the door.

Assuming it was Willow, I waved.

The door swung open.

"What are you doing here?" she asked on the other side of the screen door. "I'm sorry." She must've heard how offensive her tone was and decided to immediately apologize.

"Really," I said with a smile, "I can go. I just wanted to make sure you were okay. And I was on my way home—"

She interrupted me. "This side of town is not on your way home. I'm guessing Goldie made a special stop." She popped the door open. "Come on in. I need to count my blessings. I'm putting things away."

"Away?" I walked in and noticed there were boxes all over the place. I wanted to cheer her up, and I remembered that telling Goldie I was going to put her grandkids in the paper made her gleeful. "On my way over, I was thinking that I'd get some photos of you to feature in the paper as a contestant in the baking competition."

"Oh." She didn't seem as excited as I thought she'd be.

"Is this really an interview, or is it an 'interview'?" Willow asked. I'd told her my little secret about using my job to get in front of people and open doors to snooping.

"Only if you want it to be." I thought she was acting like a different person.

"Can I get you anything?" Willow asked over her shoulder as she led the way into the kitchen. "I'm sorry I've not unpacked all my things since the move. And now I'm not sure if I need to, since I swear I'm getting fired."

"I thought you moved here a few months ago." I recalled her mentioning she'd bought this house a few months before Mama had bought her house. It seemed a little odd for Willow to still be living out of boxes. "Where's Pete?"

I followed her to the kitchen.

"He's outside in the fenced yard. But we did move here a few months ago. I guess it was around last summer. But I've been so busy at work. I mean we had all the holidays and recently my birthday." She took a couple of glasses from a box sitting on the counter. She carried them over to the kitchen sink and ran them under the water before she filled them up. "I've only got water."

Did she not eat on dishes? Or use the glasses daily? All of this seemed very odd to me.

"Water is fine," I said and put my phone in my camera bag so I could take the glass. I was unable to stop myself from looking around. "I'm sorry I missed your birthday. Why don't we do the sip-and-clay class you were talking about as a belated birthday celebration?"

"That sounds fun." She leaned against the kitchen counter with one hand across her body while the other was propped against it with the glass. She took a sip.

"How about a few photos?" I just desperately wanted to cheer her up.

"I'm not fixed up. And I'd need to put on some makeup." She patted around her hair.

"I think you look great. But if you want, go put on some makeup, and I'll look around for some good lighting." I held the camera in my hand. "Trust me, with good lighting, you don't even need a stitch of makeup. It's a trick they teach you in journalism school."

"Okay. If you think so," she readily agreed. "Pete is in the back, so he shouldn't disturb us, and I'll just be a second."

"Okay." I started to look around the kitchen for any spots where light came in through the windows. Nothing looked good, so I walked into the family room, where the front door was located.

The last bit of the day's sunlight streamed through the bay window in the family room, the first room in the front of the house. When I looked for a chair to push up into the light, I couldn't help but notice the room had one couch, and in the corner near the white brick fireplace, a box on top of four stacked cardboard boxes was open.

Of course my snooping side didn't just stop at investigating murders.

I peeked inside the box and noticed a little clay jar that looked to be homemade. "What's this?" I muttered to myself.

It was shiny and grey, but small pieces of green glass were embedded around the middle like jewels. I looked at the jar from all angles.

My heart leapt into my throat when I noticed one of the pieces was missing. The odd shape. I dug down in the camera bag, pulled out the piece of sea glass I'd found in the office kitchen, and held it to the space on the pot.

The match was perfect.

I closed my eyes and gulped.

"Please no," I thought I whispered and looked into the box again. I moved a few odds and ends only to find a few bottles of iodine and more pieces of sea glass. The exact same color of the sea glass piece left behind.

"What did you say?" Willow called from a distance.

"I was saying you have a great spot in front of the bay." I lost my train of thought and what I was saying when I picked up a photo frame from the box to get a closer look at the picture. It was a Christmas photo taken in this very room next to the fireplace.

"Bay window!" I called out so she didn't come in to see why I'd stopped talking.

The photo was taken at Christmas because the tree was next to the mantel by the bay window. The mantel was decorated, and there were even curtains hanging up.

I put the frame back into the box and picked up a receipt from Emily's Treasures for seven chocolate bunnies. Not six like Maximus Stone had told me.

When I heard some shuffling from the hallway, I took a big step over to the bay window. I put the camera up to my eye and pretended to adjust it when she came into the room.

"What color?" she asked, holding two dresses up to her neck. "They are slightly wrinkled because I've not unpacked." She laughed. "Maybe I need an unpacking party."

"I like the sleeveless one with the high neck." I saw the floral-print dress had small buttons along the back and up to the neck, which would take her a few minutes to button, giving me a little more time to investigate the rest of the contents of the box.

"I was going to pick this one too!" she squealed and ran back. "It'll just be a minute."

"Take your time," I said. "More than you need," I whispered and went back to look in the box. "What are you up to, Willow Johnson?" I asked my inner curious journalist and picked through the box.

It seemed like she was packing to move, not unpacking to stay. She was going on the run. My mind started running down many theories about why she'd have these items and not the items pointing at the killer.

"Do you think you could help me?" Willow's voice fell off when she rounded the corner and came into the room, where she found me with the clay pot in one hand and the piece of sea glass in the other.

"I'm going to go out on a big limb here and say someone gave you this?" I asked, holding both of my hands out for her to see. "Let me make another guess." I was starting to read her body language.

Willow Johnson's facial features weren't as joyous as they were when she was excited to do the photo shoot. Quite the opposite.

Her eyes had narrowed into what I'd call a hateful stare. One that wasn't so nice. Her cheeks were indented as if all the air had been sucked out of her little body, which was now as stiff as Frances Green's.

"You killed Frances." It didn't take a scholar to put two and two together. "The iodine poisoning and the sea glass you used to cut the pane from the *Junction Journal* office door to get inside to do what? See what I had on you? The case?"

"I would ask you to leave because asking is the southern way to do things, right?" Willow's voice turned to mock mine. "Well, bless your heart." She continued to try to speak in a southern drawl. "Isn't that what y'all say when you insult someone?"

She emphasized "y'all."

"What were you going to do? Just leave town?" I asked. "Let someone else go to jail for a murder you committed? Why would you pin something like this on my mama?"

I had to throw out the personal question.

"Why?" She threw her head back and laughed. "Your mama has it in for me."

"Mama? She wouldn't hurt a flea," I spat, acting as though I was going to put the camera back in its case. "I've never heard her even mention you."

"Everything she's done since she moved here last Mother's Day she's taken from me. When I saw her in the Incubator during the sign-up for the Hip Hop Hurray Festival Bake-Off, I knew it was my time to take her out. For the good of the community. I'd already started poisoning Frances and just gave a little extra dose to the rabbit I'd bought for Maximus."

I put the camera back in the bag and remembered Chief Strickland was the last person I'd called, so I hit the redial on my phone and left it sitting in the bag.

"You premeditated killing Frances because you knew she was going to make a bunny change this year." It all started to click. "You know so much about influencers. You are in charge of Maximus Stone's social media and influencers, so if he's not making all the money, he won't need you anymore."

She started to clap as though I'd delivered a great performance.

"But how did you poison her? I didn't see your name on the lists." I wanted to hear her spill her guts just in case Matthew picked up the call.

I cast a quick glance at the phone and noticed the time was ticking away, letting me know he'd answered.

"Do you think planning a murder is easy? I knew if I needed to keep my job and slowly poison Frances in case she did what I knew she was going to do, I had to give it time." Willow had so much confidence as she paced back and forth.

Such an ego, I thought as she told her story. She was proud of it, and it made my stomach hurt. I had to hold in the feeling of nausea.

"I had told Maximus that I'd heard Frances was giving lessons, and if he wanted to give me a bonus, he should give me monthly lessons instead of cash." She smiled. "He loves money, and though he had to pay for the classes, he doesn't see that as cold hard cash. Each lesson is for four weeks. Sandy was the one who signed me up and paid for them, so it was her name on the list, not mine."

Willow Johnson had thought of everything.

"You took classes from October to just recently, based on the six p.m. piece of paper I found in her apron." How did I not think of Willow slipping the piece of paper to Frances at the Incubator and Frances putting it in the apron?

"Mm-hmmm, and it was perfect to slip an even larger amount of iodine in the chocolate bunny and dress up in one of the many costumes I have at my disposal because I keep Mr. Stone's gazillion of them. Then I hopped right over in plain sight as I put the bunny on the table, where I knew Frances would pick it up." Her eyes still on me, Willow backed up and opened the coat closet beside the door, exposing a bunny suit hanging up perfectly on a hanger. "After all, how many times have you heard from her that she can't resist a chocolate bunny?"

"Now what?" I asked her and glanced back over at the phone. The counter was gone, and my heart sank. Matthew probably couldn't hear me and hung up.

"What are you looking at?" She hurried over to the camera bag and picked up my phone.

"Paranoid?" I asked. "I'm putting the camera down, since I don't think you want to be featured in the society page after you go down to the station to confess you killed Frances Green and framed a lot of people to cover your crime." My plan was to grab my bag and get out of there.

"If you haven't noticed, I'm leaving town. I mean, look at this house." She threw her arms in the air. "This is just one example of how your *mama*," she mocked, "ruined my life. I was going to buy the house on Heart Street, but she came to town and offered Rhett Strickland all that money to buy it. She flaunted her money and got it."

"She doesn't have that much money," I said. "And that's no reason for you to have tried to frame her, which blew up in your face."

The sound of car doors slamming automatically made my shoulders fall and my body release tension.

Mere seconds later, Matthew Strickland kicked in the door, pointing a gun at Willow.

CHAPTER TWENTY

"Easter Bunny! Easter Bunny!" Children screamed over the local high school band, who played a lively rendition of "Here Comes Peter Cottontail" as they escorted the big guy.

The Easter Bunny began his own dance version while the band belted it out, and the crowd escalated their excited chatter and cheering, losing their minds with laughter and squeals of delight.

"Tickle my gizzard," Mama said. "Who knew Darren Strickland had it in 'im?" she asked the crowd. "Everyone's got on their Sunday go-to-meetin' clothes."

It made her giddy to see the village folk dressed in colorful and festive outfits, such as Easter bonnets, bunny ears, and pastel-colored clothing that went along with what you'd see at our Baptist church back home.

The loud drums, horns, and other instruments played by the band walking past saved me from commenting to her, so I just nodded.

Mama clapped to the upbeat, cheerful music and even did a little jig.

By the screaming waves of excitement, I knew Darren was getting closer. The whiz of candy being thrown into the crowd sent the little children through the spectators' legs to fight for each little piece that landed on the road.

The kids' Easter baskets were filling up with sweet treats and even small toys. Their faces lit up when they showed their parents what they'd scored.

The children jumped up and down with excitement as the Easter Bunny came into full view on the float.

"I don't think Darren is doing the wave," I leaned over and whispered to Mama when I noticed Darren was wildly waving his arms to the music and breaking into some of the crazy dance moves that he must've done to secure his spot.

I couldn't contain the joy I felt inside and out when I knew he'd seen Mama and me. The float stopped so the band could play the tune to the children's sing-along game of "Little Bunny Foo-Foo."

Darren hopped off the float and performed the song's actions as best as he could in the costume. He went down the crowd, giving high fives and fist bumps.

When he got to me, he covered his eyes and played a little peek-a-boo. I threw my head back in laughter. His big paw took my hand, and he lifted it to his furry bunny lips and pretended to kiss it.

The crowd went nuts, cheering and screaming so loudly that Darren really got into it. He twirled me around before taking me into his arms and dipping me back.

"Wow!" a lady next to me screamed in my ear when Darren had finally decided to leave me alone. "You're lucky! I've never seen the bunny do that, and my family and I have been coming here for four years."

"Are you a citizen of Holiday Junction?" I asked.

"No. We are tourists. We never miss the Hip Hop Hurray Festival." She pointed at her children, who were racing around to collect as much candy as possible, sharing their spoils with one another.

"I'm with the local newspaper, and later this afternoon, I'm working the egg-dyeing station. If you want to stop by, I bet I can get you and your family your own personal visit with the Easter Bunny, and I'd love to take your photo for the *Junction Journal*." I loved being able to make tourists happy with their visits so they'd come back.

"We would love that. Yes!" She and I exchanged the time and place to make sure we were on the same page before we dispersed now that the parade was over.

Everyone had stayed around for the final attraction, the Easter Bunny.

"How about this spot?" Kristine Whitlock asked from the booth in front of the inn where she'd scheduled for the tourists to get their photos with Mayor Paisley. "There's no better seat in the village."

"We want to thank you for saving us a spot right here." Before the parade started, Kristine had called Mama and told her she saved us a spot on the curb in front of the Jubilee Inn.

"Can I get a few shots of the mayor with tourists?" I asked, not about to let this opportunity go by.

"Absolutely." Kristine gave me her full approval. "I'll also send you all the forms." She was referring to the forms people signed when they wanted to take a photo. These forms gave tourists' consent to let the village use them for marketing and social media for Holiday Junction.

We kept the forms on file at the *Junction Journal* office in case someone came back and accused us of using a photo of them without their permission.

"Are you doing okay?" Kristine asked. "I heard about Willow Johnson. That was why I made sure to check on Millie Kay. We love you and your family. We don't want Willow Johnson's jealousy over your mama buying the house."

"We are fine. Thank you. Your kindness is greatly appreciated. I'm just glad I was able to sneak and use my phone so Chief Strickland could get to me." I wasn't sure what Willow Johnson had in store for me or if she was even going to harm me, but I knew from past experiences I couldn't chance it. "I better get some more shots because I've got to go man the egg booth for you," I said, hoping to remind her that the Jubilee Inn had sponsored the egg-dyeing station.

"Before you go," Kristine said, standing with Mama who stood next to Mayor Paisley, "do you mind going inside to snap a few of the Easter decorations? I will pay you for them. I like to put them on my social media for tourists to know we are decorated because I want them to choose the Jubilee Inn for their stay next year."

"Sure. I can snap some." I smiled and headed inside. I had no idea how much decorating Kristine had done. "How cute," I gasped when I noticed a bunny trail with a sign pointing the way.

The trail led into the room to the right, where Kristine always provided what would be considered a hospitality room with snacks and goodies. I could only imagine what she had in there for the inn's guests.

She'd made an arch of flowers around the doorframe. The vibrant yellows, oranges, and purples included Easter lilies, daffodils, tulips, Easter cactus, Gerbera daisies, irises, baby's breath, and even hyacinths.

"Beautiful." I was overwhelmed with what she'd done.

"Yes. You are." Darren surprised me. He was standing next to a table with the same flowers arranged in a vase and two taper candles flickering. "The Easter Bunny is on his lunch break, and I would love to have lunch with you."

He pulled a chair out.

"I think this is what Millie Kay said to make sure I did. Southern something or other." He smiled. "I guess if I want to date you, I have to learn manners, as your mom told me when I asked her and your father if I could take you out."

"You asked my parents?" I walked over to him with tears in my eyes.

"I did. I even looked up the manners involved in dating a southern woman. It was clear the family has to be involved." He reached over and pulled me to him. "I think learning some manners will be good for me."

He bent down and kissed me.

There was something different in me. I was changing. The more I lived in Holiday Junction, the more I felt at home in my own skin.

It hit me.

The void was no longer there. The endless running around in circles in search of the next big gig had ended. Becoming a big star was no longer a desire.

I was home.

I was finally home.

CHAPTER TWENTY-ONE

Merry Maker

Well, it looks like Diffy Delk is going to have some stiff competition coming up. From the word around town and putting my ear to the ground, I've heard Darren Strickland has gone back to college to get his law degree.

To my knowledge, he'd secretly had a year under his belt. But don't tell Chief Strickland that. Only the Merry Maker could find out that secret.

That means only one thing. Who will win the battle of the crimes and criminals in Holiday Junction? Will the son finally get revenge on his father?

May the best Strickland win.

I'm off to make the plans for our next big fun holiday. Keep your eyes and ears peeled because you never know where I'll place the next sign. It could be in your backyard.

According to what I've heard, Goldie Bennett has been giving out friendship advice to passengers, and it's led to not only our very own Violet Rhinehammer getting on the wrong side of a killer but the death of a budding friendship that was never meant to be.

The breeze that flutters off the sea and whispers of the budding romance between Violet Rhinehammer and Darren Strickland tells me Violet won't have time for a new friendship. After all, I think someone said she now has custody of a dog named Pete.

I don't think I'll be putting a Merry Maker sign on a trolley stop anytime soon. What would happen if the Merry Maker was on the opposite side of a killer?

THE END

If you enjoyed reading this book as much as I enjoyed writing it then be sure to return to the Amazon page and leave a review.

Go to Tonyakappes.com for a full reading order of my novels and while there join my newsletter. You can also find links to Facebook, Instagram and Goodreads.

Keep reading for a sneak peek of the next book in the series. Fourth of July Forgery is now available to purchase on Amazon or read for FREE in Kindle Unlimited.

Chapter One of Book Six
Fourth of July Forgery

Under the twilight sky, as the colorful sparks of fireworks danced above, the quaint town of Holiday Junction came alive with a symphony of laughter, joy, and the captivating warmth of an ocean breeze to celebrate the first day of the Fourth of July Festival.

I was perched at my desk in the *Junction Journal* office, overlooking the bustling scene unfolding outside. The ocean's salty aroma wafted through the open windows, mingling with the excitement and anticipation that hung in the air.

"Violet, are you 'bout done?" my mama, Millie Kaye, asked. She was southern to her core and brimmed with enthusiasm for any celebration that came our way.

She popped her head into the door of my office.

I had to keep myself from laughing as I took in an outfit I'd call gaudy, but she'd call it getting into the spirit of the Fourth of July.

Mama had carefully selected an ensemble that exuded patriotic flair. She wore a flowy navy-blue maxi dress adorned with white stars, its fabric swaying gently as she headed straight over to my desk with something in her fingers.

The dress was cinched at the waist with a vibrant red belt, which added a touch of boldness to her ensemble. She had a straw hat tucked underneath her arm.

"I've got my brochures just in time." She wagged the object in the air and handed it to me, giving me an even better look at it—a pair of dazzling earrings crafted in the shape of sparkling fireworks. Her pocketbook was in the crook of her elbow.

The earrings dangled delicately, each burst capturing the essence of the celebratory fireworks that would soon light up the night sky.

"Look at what a bang-up job Clara and Garrett did down at the Printing Press." She pointed at the front of the brochure, showing that even her nails had fireworks painted on them. "We bartered."

She was lit up like a sparkler at the memory of making this deal.

"And what did you agree upon, Mama?" I asked.

"They gave me a steep discount on the printing in full color, and I gave them three months of free membership at the Leisure Center." Mama popped the straw hat on top of her head.

The hat was adorned with a wide red ribbon. A small American flag pin was pinned on the ribbon, a subtle yet powerful symbol of her patriotism.

She snapped the top of her purse open, took out a handful of the brochures, and slapped them down on my desk.

"Now, me and you are going to be giving these out tonight," she told me with a warm smile and a twinkle in her eye.

"Okay, Mama." I got up and noticed her comfortable-looking yet stylish white sandals adorned with red and blue accents.

It was Mama's way of having the perfect balance between fashion and practicality, ensuring she could navigate the festivities with ease. Mama never did anything without thinking through the outfit she would wear for any event.

"You aren't going out there lookin' like that, are you?" she asked. Then she must have realized what she'd said, because she gasped slightly and knotted her brows. "You look all right. Besides, it's getting dark out soon. And, well"—her lips pinched—"everyone will be looking at the fireworks instead of you."

That was Mama's way of apologizing. Her southern way. I'd gotten used to it over the years. She loved me, and I knew it, or she'd never have followed me to Holiday Junction when I moved here a little over a year ago. Just about a month later, she showed up at my door with her suitcase in hand, just landed from our home in Normal, Kentucky.

I figured she was going to stay for one week, maybe two. Boy, was I wrong. She not only stayed but ended up buying a house. Then my daddy moved here. Soon, she started working with me at the *Junction Journal*.

Now she was opening up the Leisure Center because she said

Holiday Junction needed a place for seniors to go, though she refused to call it that.

"I'm not going to say anything, but I love the you-know-what." Her words ran together.

"Mama," I said in a tone that told her not to say another word.

"I know, I know." She sighed. "I'm going to use the ladies' room, so get your stuff and let's go."

"Yeah, yeah." When I walked over to get my camera bag, I stopped at the window and looked out at the beach.

As I gazed out of the office window, my heart fluttered with excitement and anticipation. The Fourth of July festivities were in full swing, and as the co-Merry Maker of Holiday Junction with Darren Strickland, it was my responsibility to ensure the holiday celebration's grand finale was nothing short of spectacular.

The Merry Maker was one of the most important jobs, if not *the* most important, in Holiday Junction, and it was secret. No one, well, no one but Darren, Mama, Vern McKenna, and I knew we were the current Merry Makers.

Darren, with his warm smile and unwavering enthusiasm, was not only my partner in merrymaking but also someone with whom I had developed a budding relationship.

We shared a deep connection and a love for this charming town. It was no surprise that he called the lighthouse his home, a symbol of guidance and strength that overlooked the picturesque coastline.

Together, Darren and I had meticulously planned the holiday's last hurrah, a gathering that would bring the townsfolk together for one final moment of joy and camaraderie.

Our chosen location for this year's festivities was the beach, and to mark the spot, we had placed a magnificent ten-foot sparkly rocket that shone and shimmered in the fading daylight. Vern had made the rocket for us using his amazing skills as a carpenter.

This iconic symbol of the large rocket held a special meaning for the townspeople, signifying that the heart of the celebration would unfold right here, where the crashing waves met the sandy shore. In this place, laughter would echo, memories would be made, and the spirit of community would be ignited.

As the sun began its descent, casting a warm golden glow across the beach, I couldn't help but feel a swell of pride. The atmosphere crackled with anticipation, and the townsfolk knew, without a doubt, that this was the place to be, the epicenter of the evening's revelry.

Children ran along the shoreline, their laughter mixing with the sound of crashing waves. Families set up picnic blankets, their mouths watering in anticipation of the delicious food and sweet treats that would be shared. The air was filled with the cheerful chatter of friends and neighbors, the people's faces painted with expressions of joy and excitement.

"You ready?" Mama asked, bringing me out of the nostalgia I'd entered. "Violet?"

"Yep." I grabbed the camera bag from the shelf and turned around. "I'm going to get some great photos for tomorrow's special Fourth of July edition of the *Junction Journal.*"

Mama led me all the way down the sidewalk in front of all the seaside shops, giving her brochures to anyone who extended a hand.

"Darlin', can you believe the turnout we're havin' for the Fourth of July festivities?" Mama exclaimed, her eyes sparkling with joy.

She'd stopped at Popcorn Paradise. The food stand offered a variety of popcorn flavors, from traditional buttery popcorn to gourmet options like caramel, cheese, and even spicy flavors.

"The fireworks display is gonna be a real showstopper this year, and I'm hopin' folks will come check out the Leisure Center while they're at it." Mama turned and looked back over her shoulder to see what I was staring at. "Do you want some popcorn?"

"I think I will, so you go on and I'll meet you at the Merry Maker sign," I suggested because she clearly wanted to hand out all those brochures.

"Don't forget to hand those out. I don't want to see a single one in your hand when I meet you." She made sure I understood what she expected of me before she took off down the sidewalk.

As I stood in line, I couldn't help but take out my camera to snap a few candid shots of children eating some of the festival foods. The kids were sitting on the curb of the street that had been blocked off by the Holiday Junction Police Department.

My mouth watered when I realized I was next in line, and my eyes focused on the caramel popcorn option.

"One small caramel popcorn, please," I told the young man who asked to take my order. He stood behind a small screen window barely cracked open.

"Make it a large," a familiar voice boomed behind me. The speaker's hand placed a ten-dollar bill in the sliding window.

With a contented sigh, I turned to Darren. Our eyes met for a brief moment, sharing unspoken understanding and excitement.

"I've been looking for you." His dark eyes framed by his thick brows sent my heart into a crazy butterfly spiral. He raised his other hand, which held the Leisure Center brochure. "I saw Millie Kay. She said you were at Popcorn Paradise."

"I'm so glad you found me." I tried to keep my smile small, but it was as large as the fireworks display would be. He looked so cute in his brown longboard-style shorts, loose long-sleeved white shirt with the sleeves rolled up, and dock shoes.

He was so laid-back with his dressing style and long hair that he was good for me.

I took the popcorn from the guy behind the window. Darren and I stepped away from the stand.

"Look around at all the happy faces." He took a handful of caramel popcorn, popping a few kernels in his mouth.

"We did good this time." I shoved a handful of the delicious treat in my mouth, agreeing we'd finally found a good rhythm for where the secret Merry Maker spot for each holiday would be hosted. Previously, we'd never agreed on where they should be.

With mouths full of popcorn, Darren and I took the moment to glance at our surroundings. This was our way to bring happiness and unity to the people we cherished.

159

Together, we'd create a night to remember, a night when the spirit of the Fourth of July would shine as brightly as the stars above us.

"Let's go get a front-row beach seat," Darren said. He started to lead me down the road to the big wooden rocket, walking with the rest of the crowd.

We took our time so I could stop and snap photos of all the food vendors.

The Beachside Grill was a cute stand that served juicy burgers, hot dogs, and smoky barbecued chicken. Everything there looked like it was expertly cooked to perfection.

Seafood Shack was another cute stand serving fresh catches from the ocean and a variety of other seafood delights, from succulent shrimp skewers and crispy fish tacos to creamy clam chowder and mouthwatering lobster rolls. The owners boasted that seafood lovers were in for a delectable treat.

"You can wash that down with one of those." I pointed at the Lemonade Oasis stand and watched Darren scarf down a shrimp skewer.

Of course, there was a booth for people who wanted more sweets than the caramel popcorn stand offered.

Sweet Treats Delight had a display of cotton candy, caramel apples, chocolate-dipped strawberries, and colorful candy floss. You could imagine how long the line was when we walked past.

"I think I got some really good candids for the morning paper." I quickly flipped through the digital photos to show Darren before we took off our shoes and walked on the sandy beach.

"It's really crowded." Darren had stopped. He towered over almost everyone's heads as he looked over them to see if we could get a closer spot. "I say we go up there." He raised his chin in the air.

I looked up to see where he was pointing.

"I'm up for it." I turned the camera off and put it back in the bag so it didn't get sandy on our way to his lighthouse. The perfect view of the fireworks would be from the tip-top of that structure.

With a touch of excitement lingering in the air, Darren and I climbed the winding staircase from inside his house.

"We better hurry." Darren was ahead of me, holding a six-pack of beer he'd grabbed out of his refrigerator on our way to the steps. "I can hear the booms."

As we reached the top, the vibrant colors of the Fourth of July fireworks painted the night sky above the ocean, creating a breathtaking spectacle.

Darren had a mischievous glint in his eyes as he handed me a couple of chilled beers. Condensation glistened on the bottles. We settled ourselves on the platform, our legs dangling over the side, feeling the cool ocean breeze against our skin.

As the first fireworks exploded above us, we clinked our bottles together in a toast, savoring the fizzy anticipation that mirrored the sparkling lights overhead. The symphony of crackling bursts and whistling trails filled the night, punctuated by gasps and applause from the crowd below.

I couldn't help but feel a sense of awe and gratitude as we sat there, witnessing the colorful bursts of light illuminating the darkness. The waves' rhythmic pounding against the shore added a soothing backdrop to the spectacle, creating a moment of pure enchantment.

"I better snap a few photos." I put my beer bottle down and dragged the bag closer to me.

The photos would be beautiful but nothing like being there in person.

"That should be enough." I wanted to make sure I was present for the rest of photos and satisfied I'd gotten a few good ones to use.

We leaned back against the sturdy structure of the lighthouse, our gazes fixed on the mesmerizing display. Darren's presence beside me brought a warmth and comfort that I had come to cherish while we marveled at the magic unfolding before our eyes.

As the fireworks painted the night sky with cascades of red, white, and blue, the world seemed to fade away, leaving only Darren, the lights, and me. Our laughter and whispered conversations filled the space between the bursts. We shared stories and dreams amidst the symphony of colors.

Time seemed to stand still as we basked in the beauty of the moment. The stars above seemed to twinkle with delight, as if they were joining in the celebration of this special night.

With each explosion, I felt a sense of unity, not only with Darren but also with the entire town of Holiday Junction. It was a moment of collective awe, a shared experience that transcended individual differences and brought us together under the magic of the fireworks.

As the grand finale erupted in a shower of shimmering sparks, we sat in silence, our hearts filled with gratitude and wonder. The sounds of the cheers and applause from the crowd below reached our ears, a testament to the joy and delight the fireworks had brought to everyone in Holiday Junction.

Then some screaming suddenly took over the cheers. Darren and I stood up to see why.

"What's going on?" I asked, leaning over the railing.

As a journalist with an insatiable curiosity, I couldn't help but dart off back down the stairs to get an up-close and personal photo of whatever was going on.

I took a deep breath, allowing the salty breeze to fill my lungs, heightening my senses. The stage was set, the atmosphere charged with anticipation.

Little did I know that by the end of this night, the vibrant celebration would give way to a grim discovery, plunging Holiday Junction into a web of secrets and intrigue.

As soon as we reached the beach, one last burst of fireworks illuminated the darkening sky, and I felt a surge of adrenaline, knowing that my nose for news and the light of the fireworks would lead me straight into the heart of the unfolding mystery.

At the time, I didn't realize it was a dead body on the beach.

Fourth of July Forgery is now available to purchase or in Kindle Unlimited.

BOOKS BY TONYA
SOUTHERN HOSPITALITY WITH A SMIDGEN OF HOMICIDE

Camper & Criminals Cozy Mystery Series

All is good in the camper-hood until a dead body shows up in the woods.

BEACHES, BUNGALOWS, AND BURGLARIES
DESERTS, DRIVING, & DERELICTS
FORESTS, FISHING, & FORGERY
CHRISTMAS, CRIMINALS, AND CAMPERS
MOTORHOMES, MAPS, & MURDER
CANYONS, CARAVANS, & CADAVERS
HITCHES, HIDEOUTS, & HOMICIDES
ASSAILANTS, ASPHALT & ALIBIS
VALLEYS, VEHICLES & VICTIMS
SUNSETS, SABBATICAL AND SCANDAL
TENTS, TRAILS AND TURMOIL
KICKBACKS, KAYAKS, AND KIDNAPPING
GEAR, GRILLS & GUNS
EGGNOG, EXTORTION, AND EVERGREEN
ROPES, RIDDLES, & ROBBERIES
PADDLERS, PROMISES & POISON
INSECTS, IVY, & INVESTIGATIONS
OUTDOORS, OARS, & OATH
WILDLIFE, WARRANTS, & WEAPONS
BLOSSOMS, BBQ, & BLACKMAIL
LANTERNS, LAKES, & LARCENY
JACKETS, JACK-O-LANTERN, & JUSTICE
SANTA, SUNRISES, & SUSPICIONS
VISTAS, VICES, & VALENTINES
ADVENTURE, ABDUCTION, & ARREST
RANGERS, RVS, & REVENGE

CAMPFIRES, COURAGE & CONVICTS
TRAPPING, TURKEY & THANKSGIVING
GIFTS, GLAMPING & GLOCKS
ZONING, ZEALOTS, & ZIPLINES
HAMMOCKS, HANDGUNS, & HEARSAY
QUESTIONS, QUARRELS, & QUANDARY
WITNESS, WOODS, & WEDDING
ELVES, EVERGREENS, & EVIDENCE
MOONLIGHT, MARSHMALLOWS, & MANSLAUGHTER
BONFIRE, BACKPACKS, & BRAWLS

Killer Coffee Cozy Mystery Series

Welcome to the Bean Hive Coffee Shop where the gossip is just as hot as the coffee.

SCENE OF THE GRIND
MOCHA AND MURDER
FRESHLY GROUND MURDER
COLD BLOODED BREW
DECAFFEINATED SCANDAL
A KILLER LATTE
HOLIDAY ROAST MORTEM
DEAD TO THE LAST DROP
A CHARMING BLEND NOVELLA (CROSSOVER WITH MAGICAL CURES MYSTERY)
FROTHY FOUL PLAY
SPOONFUL OF MURDER
BARISTA BUMP-OFF
CAPPUCCINO CRIMINAL
MACCHIATO MURDER

Holiday Cozy Mystery Series

A CHARMING SPELL
A CHARMING MAGIC
A CHARMING SECRET
A CHARMING CHRISTMAS (novella)
A CHARMING FATALITY
A CHARMING DEATH (novella)
A CHARMING GHOST
A CHARMING HEX
A CHARMING VOODOO
A CHARMING CORPSE
A CHARMING MISFORTUNE
A CHARMING BLEND (CROSSOVER WITH A KILLER COFFEE COZY)
A CHARMING DECEPTION

Mail Carrier Cozy Mystery Series

Welcome to Sugar Creek Gap where more than the mail is being delivered.

STAMPED OUT
ADDRESS FOR MURDER
ALL SHE WROTE
RETURN TO SENDER
FIRST CLASS KILLER
POST MORTEM
DEADLY DELIVERY
RED LETTER SLAY

About Tonya

Tonya has written over 100 novels, all of which have graced numerous bestseller lists, including the USA Today. Best known for stories charged with emotion and humor and filled with flawed characters, her novels have garnered reader praise and glowing critical reviews. She lives with her husband and a very spoiled rescue cat named Ro. Tonya grew up in the small southern Kentucky town of Nicholasville. Now that her four boys are grown men, Tonya writes full-time in her camper she calls her SHAMPER (she-camper).

Learn more about her be sure to check out her website tonyakappes.com. Find her on Facebook, Twitter, BookBub, and Instagram

Sign up to receive her newsletter, where you'll get free books, exclusive bonus content, and news of her releases and sales.

If you liked this book, please take a few minutes to leave a review now! Authors (Tonya included) really appreciate this, and it helps draw more readers to books they might like. Thanks!

Cover artist: Mariah Sinclair: The Cover Vault

Made in the USA
Coppell, TX
15 November 2023